With Samuel prop~~~~~~~~~~~~~~~~~~~~~~~~~~ applied pressure to the wound a~~~~~~~~~~~~~~~~~~~~~~

"Two men," Samuel whispered, "two men held up the stage. They killed Billy's father. Shot the driver in the arm. Remember this, so you can collect the reward."

"What reward?"

"Tell the sheriff and the reward money will pay off my debts," Samuel wheezed, "so Sarah can keep the farm." His eyes welled with tears.

"Take it easy. You need to rest." Mark applied more pressure.

"A dark birthmark under his ear." Samuel started to shake.

"Who?" Mark asked.

"Billy," Samuel panted.

"Oh, Samuel, why you? That damn canteen. It should be me laying here. Why, God? Why Samuel?"

"Collect the reward. Promise. Sarah needs the money."

Mark nodded.

Samuel closed his eyes for a moment then murmured, "Blood money, she'd call it. Don't tell her I killed two men. No violence."

"No violence," Mark repeated. "She knows you would never kill anyone. You were defending yourself. "Are you sure you don't want me to tell her?"

Samuel nodded.

"Then she'll never know." Mark assured him.

"Promise."

"Yes, I promise. She'll never know the truth about the robbery or the killing."

"Please take care of them."

"Yes, Samuel. Don't worry. I'll take care of them."

Book One: Settler's Life

by

Judy Sharer

A Plains Life Series

This is a work of fiction. Names, characters, places, and incidents are either the product of the author's imagination or are used fictitiously, and any resemblance to actual persons living or dead, business establishments, events, or locales, is entirely coincidental.

Settler's Life

COPYRIGHT © 2018 by Judy M Sharer

All rights reserved. No part of this book may be used or reproduced in any manner whatsoever without written permission of the author or The Wild Rose Press, Inc. except in the case of brief quotations embodied in critical articles or reviews.
Contact Information: info@thewildrosepress.com

Cover Art by *Diana Carlile*

The Wild Rose Press, Inc.
PO Box 708
Adams Basin, NY 14410-0708
Visit us at www.thewildrosepress.com

Publishing History
First Cactus Rose Edition, 2018
Print ISBN 978-1-5092-2098-4
Digital ISBN 978-1-5092-2099-1

A Plains Life
Published in the United States of America

Dedication

Dedicated to Johanna Sayre my dear friend and the members of my writer's groups for their positive encouragement and never-ending support.

Chapter One

The icy winds of the Kansas winter evening seeped through Sarah's thin coat and left its chill. She pulled the garment tighter, closed her eyes, and took a deep breath, as she cradled her arms to her chest. *Oh, how my arms long to hold little Walter again. If only the fever hadn't overcome me.* She so wanted to give Samuel another son.

Now, two months to the day since her baby passed, Sarah Clark bent down to trace her fingers over the wooden marker her husband lovingly carved for their son's gravesite. "Walter Samuel Clark, Born January 10, 1858, Died January 10, 1858." Sarah's voice quivered as she read.

Sarah's long auburn hair, usually coiled on her head, hadn't been cared for since the baby died. Typically, she and the children vied in spelling bees, worked on projects, practiced handwriting or drilled times tables together during the day. But now her memory of the lifeless child consumed her every waking minute.

Chilled, she returned to the farmhouse to make a cup of tea. As she sat cradling the steaming cup in her hands, she watched Samuel playing checkers with their daughter Lydia while older brother Jack looked on, eager to play the winner. When the games were over, the children readied for bed and climbed the ladder to the sleeping loft followed by Samuel.

Sarah overheard Samuel praying with Jack and then with Lydia who slept on the other side behind hanging blankets in her "bedroom."

"Sweet dreams," Samuel told the children, then climbed down and walked to his wife.

He rubbed his arms, sore from chopping wood, then bent down and gently wrapped them around Sarah's shoulders and kissed her cheek.

Sarah tensed at his touch.

"Are you coming to bed?"

"Not right now. You go ahead."

"Don't stay up too late, sweetheart. The bed is cold without you beside me."

How could she explain to her husband of thirteen years that she ached to hold her infant son in her arms, or why she silently cried herself to sleep at night? How could she share the reason she couldn't bear Samuel's tender touch or look into his soft brown eyes? Sarah couldn't let go of the memory of Samuel handing her their limp, lifeless baby. The child she envisioned cried, breathed, and was full of energy. Angry at God, sorry for her family's loss, and guilt-ridden for taking ill, Sarah began to weep.

She wasn't able to sleep, for every time she closed her eyes, her mind focused on her sweet baby's face. Walter's tiny little fingers and toes were perfect. His hair was brown like his father's. She longed to see him smile, hear him cry, have him suckle. Sarah took another sip of tea, then dipped her pen in ink to write the letter that needed to be written two months ago. *If only Mother lived closer.* She longed to hear her mother's voice and ached for another woman's compassion.

March 7, 1858
Northwest Border, Riley County Kansas

Dearest Mother,
I wish I had good news, but there is no way to say this other than what happened was God's will. We lost our baby.
When I took ill with fever, I feared for our child. Samuel never left my side until the morning of the third day, January 10th, when we lost our boy. We named him Walter Samuel Clark. I so wish you were here, Mother.

Sarah paused in her writing. *Taking Walter away wasn't fair. Not a defenseless child. Why? Why me? Why my family?* A tear formed and she brushed it away.

If only the fever had not overtaken me. That sharp, stabbing pain in my stomach the likes of which I've never dealt with before, lasted several hours and I knew something was terribly wrong. I was so weak Samuel worried he would lose us both. I do not know why the Lord did not answer my prayers and let me keep my baby. It is hard to comprehend His ways, yet I realize I must. My heart aches still.

A vision of standing beside the hastily dug grave, staring at the ground that would close out the light of the world above, flashed before her. *Was tiny Walter wrapped in enough quilts to keep him warm? Does he know he is loved and missed? Will we meet again in Heaven? He never got to see my face. How will he know I am his mother?* She sighed, dipped her pen, and continued.

Samuel built a beautiful little coffin. We buried Walter beside his uncle Richard under the old elm tree. I wanted him to rest in peace as quickly as possible.

3

The day was cold and blustery when Samuel cleared the snow to build a fire to thaw the ground enough to pick and shovel a shallow grave; a grave he will dig deeper when the ground is soft again come spring.

I have not wanted to do much since then. Emptiness and ashamed are all I feel inside. I see the pain on Samuel's face although he tries to hide it. But I understand for I feel the same loss. Samuel said we would try again, but I am not sure I can endure the pain of losing another child.

Suddenly Sarah gasped, *Samuel's mother needs to be told too. Perhaps it would be easier for her to hear from Mother rather than reading the sad news in a letter. Maybe Mother should tell her in person.*

She continued.

Would you please tell Polly about her grandson's death? My mind will rest at ease knowing his mother received the news from you in person rather than in a letter.

I wish Emma and Matthew were already on their way to live with us. Your grandchildren wait anxiously to see their aunt and uncle again.

It is late and Samuel is already in bed, so I will close now. I miss you, Mother. Please write soon.

Your loving daughter,

Sarah

A tear trickling down Sarah's cheek splashed on the paper as she folded the letter and wax sealed the envelope. Now was the time to return to her responsibilities and care for her loving family. She would never forget little Walter. The loss of her child would always be with her, his tombstone a reminder of the ache in her heart that would never go away.

Writing to her mother placed her life back into perspective. With family members coming to stay and all the work ahead of them in the next few months, she couldn't dwell on her loss anymore. It wasn't her loss alone...all the family grieved. She hadn't been there for them in their time of need, especially Jack and Lydia.

Earlier in the day she assisted with the birth of a calf. Sarah took the event as a sign to trust again in God. After seeing life come into the world a new stirring of hope enveloped her. She looked toward the future as a new beginning. Sarah looked at life as a book and understood the time had come to turn the page and begin a new chapter. She climbed into bed, snuggled against the small of Samuel's back for warmth, and said a prayer for brighter days ahead.

****

The following morning, Samuel woke first and dressed quietly, trying not to wake Sarah. When he walked past the kitchen table, he noticed the envelope addressed to her mother. He grabbed the bucket from the kitchen and headed out the door to fetch water. Sarah was in the kitchen starting breakfast when he returned.

"Good morning, dear," Samuel said, noticing her hair neatly combed into a bun and pinned on top of her head. Something had changed. "Did my getting out of bed wake you?"

"No, besides, it's time I get our family back to our regular routine. Now go work up an appetite. We're having one of your favorites for breakfast- sausage and gravy over biscuits." She patted him on the back and gave him a gentle nudge toward the door.

Filling the final bucket of water for the animals,

Samuel glanced over at the almost empty corncrib beside the south side of the barn. The family endured a long cold winter but survived. He remembered when his best friend Mark Hewitt visited last year and they built the corncrib together.

Mark also helped build the barn, as well as the small corral and chicken coop. Samuel usually saved larger projects on the farm for Mark's visits. There was still much work to be done, so it was a good thing he was due to arrive soon.

Samuel was anxious to ride into Dead Flats to meet Mark. He sent a letter last fall asking if Mark could help with some building projects and heavier chores come spring like digging out the root cellar. Mark usually visited once or twice a year if he could. This visit, Samuel wanted Mark's presence and storytelling to lift the spirits of the family again.

The two men grew up and attended school together in Pennsylvania. They're as close as brothers. Mark's visits to the farm always means good times plus help with the heavy work and of course anything Sarah needed or wanted done.

"Pa!" The sound of his son's voice jolted Samuel out of his reverie.

"Ma has breakfast ready," Jack announced, as he ran out to stand beside his poppa. "She said to wash up and come in." Jack glanced at the empty corncrib. "A tough year is ahead, isn't it, Pa?"

"We'll make it." Samuel's assurances sounded strained and hollow to his ears. Then he put his arm around his son's shoulders and drew him close. "Are you getting taller, son?" Samuel tried to change the subject.

"Almost five-foot, four inches, according to Ma, although we haven't measured in a while. Maybe I'm even taller now since my twelfth birthday." Jack stood straight like a soldier at attention.

"A few more inches and you'll catch up to me." Samuel gave Jack's shoulder a quick squeeze. "As I'm sure you've heard, Mark is coming. We'll be back in two days in time for supper. You can handle the chores by yourself for a few days can't you, son? You're growing up a fine young man."

"Sure, chores aren't a problem, Pa. Lydia and I like it when Mark comes. His stories are full of adventure and excitement. He gets in some real trouble sometimes, doesn't he, Pa? Like the time the sheriff threw him in jail for shooting a prairie rattler in town while sitting in the barber's chair. He tells different stories every visit."

"Yes, indeed, he does tell a good story." Samuel set the bucket on the ground. "Come on, Jack, we better get in for breakfast or your Ma will skin us alive. We can finish with the animals afterward."

Inside, Lydia, a curly-haired redhead the spitting image of her mother and with her father's dimples, helped place the food on the table. Everyone sat and bowed their heads as Lydia asked the blessing.

She bowed her head and recited the breakfast prayer, "Bless us O Lord, and these Thy gifts which we are about to receive from Thy bounty through Christ, Our Lord. Amen." Then the family loaded up on hot-from-the-oven biscuits made from the dwindling supply of flour smothered with sausage gravy.

Breakfast chores finished, Samuel sat beside Sarah as they wrote out lists. Sarah listed provisions needed to tide them over until the fall harvest. Now only the second week of March and already they were running low on staples like salt, flour, and cornmeal. Next, she made a list of the kitchen garden seeds she would need to plant when the weather became warmer. She compared her list to last year's and increased the amounts to allow for her two siblings' arrival later in the summer. Samuel's list contained supplies needed for the repairs he planned to complete during Mark's visit.

They included rebuilding the chicken coop after heavy snow toppled the old one, adding to the corncrib, and enlarging the root cellar with shelves large enough to hold the pickling crocks and produce from Sarah's garden. Then, if time permitted, the men would tackle Sarah's smaller projects like a shelf for the kitchen and a bedside table.

Samuel needed bountiful crops this year so they wouldn't lose as many head of cattle the next winter. Last year's harvest hadn't produced as he planned. The fields yielded only two cuttings. This year, he'd clear more land and plant additional corn if his credit held at the hardware and general store.

Chapter Two

The family gathered in the kitchen for their good-byes as Samuel detailed last minute instructions with Jack. "Please keep the animals feed and watered, put corn out for the chickens and milk the cow for your ma, Jack." Samuel smiled and gave each child a warm hug and kiss.

Sarah followed him outside and held out her letter and coin for the stamp. "Will you mail this for me, Samuel? It's a letter to my mother telling her about the baby and asking her to tell your mother for us."

"Of course, sweetheart," Samuel said, placing the letter inside his coat pocket for safe keeping. He packed his gear in the wagon along with the food Sarah fixed, kissed her lovingly, and asked one last time, "Are you sure you don't need anything before I leave, Sarah?"

"No, we'll be fine." Sarah stepped closer, then cupped his face in her hands and kissed him.

Samuel hugged her close and kissed her again before beginning his day and a half journey to Dead Flats. He was happy to see the old Sarah he knew returning to him at last.

As he rode, Samuel glanced at the clouds as they drifted overhead, but always had one eye on the hunt for supper. The solitude of the day provided him time to pray and reflect on his current situation while a lucky shot bagged him a grouse.

When Samuel arrived at the cluster of old oak trees marking the spot where the family always camped on their way to town, his stomach started to complain. Before building a fire he unhitched, tethered, and fed his horse, Button.

He then kindled a fire of dried grass and twigs from a limb of an old oak not strong enough to survive the long cold winter. He stared at the sky as the sun sank to the horizon and then out of sight as he ate the biscuits Sarah packed for him along with the roasted grouse. Strong hot coffee provided welcome warmth on the chilly March evening.

As the campfire died, Samuel lay in his bedroll in the back of the wagon looking up at the night sky. He caught glimpses of the moon as thin clouds rolled past. Babbling noises from the nearby creek soon lulled him to sleep.

The next morning there was a chill in the air when the sound of birds chattering and a light breeze rustling dry leaves awakened him. It hadn't snowed in two weeks and all indications pointed to an early spring thaw. He'd slept well and the fresh air and sounds of nature made him feel at peace. Warm and comfortable in his bedroll, he reluctantly crawled out, with a half-day ride to town still ahead.

He watered and fed his horse and rekindled the campfire to warm last night's coffee which he drank while enjoying a couple of Sarah's biscuits. Ready for the day, he kicked dirt on the campfire, hitched the horse to the wagon, and took off for town.

Sarah's list of provisions in his pocket was a worry. What if the storeowner wouldn't let him charge the supplies? He couldn't pay off his bill last fall and now carried only half the money needed to pay for the spring seed. Difficult times lay ahead until harvest.

Arriving at the town of Dead Flats, Samuel looked up and down the main street, but saw no sign of Mark. The town clock over the entrance of the bank chimed nine times. The letter said they'd meet mid-morning at the dry goods store.

He sure hoped Mark received his letter. Sarah and the children would be disappointed if he returned home alone. The last Samuel heard, Mark worked part-time at a hardware store in Missouri.

Samuel stopped the wagon in front of the hardware and was about to walk to the stables to check on the price of cattle when Mark got off his horse down the street.

He called out, "Mark! Good to see you, old friend! How was your ride?"

Mark turned and waved. "Good to see you too, Samuel! The ride on old Ruby seemed longer this time." He patted his mare on the neck.

Samuel walked over and shook his hand. "Sure glad you could come."

"It took the past five days to get here. But a visit with you and your family is always worth the ride. Now let's eat!" Mark stretched and yawned.

Mark stood about six feet with broad shoulders and a lean, muscular torso from years of hard work as a cowhand. His shoulder length wavy brown hair, brown eyes, and small scar on his left cheek caused people to look twice and told them Mark was definitely not the person to pick a fight with in a dark alley. Deep down, however, Mark Hewitt was a gentle, caring man.

Walking toward the restaurant Mark slapped

Samuel on the shoulder. "Hey, congratulations on becoming a father again. How are Sarah and the baby doing? Did she have a boy or a girl?"

"Jack and Lydia are fine," Samuel said, "but, Sarah took a fever and lost the baby in January. I thought I might lose her too. She blamed herself for our loss. She's doing much better now, thank goodness." At least Samuel prayed that was true. He worried about Sarah slipping back into that dark place while he was away. The past two months were trying times. It was God's will, but their loss would always be a part of them. "Sarah wants another child, at least she did."

"Gosh, sorry about the baby, Samuel. Glad to hear Sarah's doing better. How about you?"

"There are times when things are tough. Money's a bit short right now. Last fall's crops didn't fare as well as we'd hoped. But, we're managing."

"If you're short on cash, breakfast is on me. Let's go over to the hotel and get some grub."

"Are you sure?" Samuel said. "Not sure when you'll get your money back, Mark. There's no extra."

As they headed toward the hotel, Mark put his arm around Samuel's shoulder. "That's okay. This one's on me."

"You wouldn't believe the bad luck we've endured this past year," Samuel said, taking a sip of steaming coffee. "The weather didn't help. We couldn't get a third cutting of hay and the long, cold winter took a toll on the herd. In November there were nine head, but now only five. We butchered two in early February when we were running out of feed, we lost one to starvation, and traded one."

"Sorry to hear that, Samuel." Mark nodded.

"Starvation is hard to deal with while praying the cattle will make it and knowing there's a chance they won't. Right now, we have plenty of meat, but staples to feed the family until the summer crops come in are running low. Hopefully they'll let me charge a few supplies and pay only half for the seed we'll need for this year's garden and crops. Having to charge on my bill again isn't good. In fact, they may not give me credit. Without seed we may as well return to Pennsylvania." Samuel put his fork down and took another sip of coffee.

"Don't worry," Mark said. "Your supplies today are on me in exchange for letting me stay a couple of weeks. Sarah's cooking is better than mine any day."

"Thanks, Mark. You have no idea how much that helps. We don't need a lot. We'll pay you back when we sell a few extra bags of grain this fall, depending if the weather is good and we get three, maybe even four cuttings."

Mark nodded again. "Glad to help."

The men lingered over their breakfast of flapjacks and sausage while enjoying the warmth of the restaurant and the pleasure of each other's company. Standing to leave, Samuel said, "Sarah sent along a letter, so I'll head to the postal office and we can meet at the dry goods store."

"Do what you need. See you there." Mark finished his coffee as Samuel headed out the door.

At the dry goods store, Samuel placed items from Sarah's list onto the counter for the storekeeper to tally.

Mark walked in with a newspaper under his arm and asked the owner for a couple of cigars and to fill two sacks of candy for Jack and Lydia.

Samuel reluctantly let Mark pay the bill and asked for the amount owed on his account.

"Your balance is thirty-one dollars." The clerk wrote the number on a piece of paper and handed the paper to Samuel.

"Thanks." Samuel sighed and placed it in his coin pouch.

They loaded the provisions in the wagon. The next stop was the hardware to pick up the seed Samuel ordered last fall plus filling Sarah's kitchen garden seed list. Samuel paid for half of the order and Mark paid the rest, leaving a balance of twenty-seven dollars. *A third cutting sure would help this year if the weather cooperates or we'll have to sell our entire herd to pay off our debt come fall.* Worry seeped into the pleasure of being with Mark, but the reality was this year crops would be a deciding factor for his family.

Other folks were in the same situation with debt weighing heavy on their shoulders. Samuel's mother raised him with the principle that, if you don't have the money to pay for something, you don't buy it. He wasn't sure how he would make ends meet, however his family endured this far and they would survive. After loading the wagon, Samuel and Mark rode out of town.

"We have a whole year's worth of catching up to do," Samuel said. "You're staying for more than a couple of weeks, aren't you? Sarah would like you to stay and maybe we could get in some hunting this time. Maybe a deer for Easter and a turkey for Thanksgiving. It's odd, but they are celebrated only a week apart in April this year. You can stay at least until then, right."

"Well…" Mark started to say.

Samuel cut him off. "There's another important reason for you to stay, Mark. You see, when we buried the baby, the ground was frozen, so I built a fire to thaw the dirt enough to dig a shallow grave. In a few weeks, the ground will be soft enough to dig a real grave to bury him right. Could you stay until then? Your staying would mean a lot to Sarah and me. I don't want this to set Sarah back again. Her pain and grief have left her drained."

"Well, there's no work for me until the beginning of May, so staying as long as you want or until Sarah kicks me out isn't a problem."

"Oh, Sarah won't kick you out"—Samuel chuckled—"but you better prepare yourself. The children plan to ask you lots of questions. All they've talked about since I told them you might come are the stories you'll tell them."

"Talking is my life." Mark chuckled. "Remember how talking used to get me in trouble when we were in school?" The two men laughed out loud recalling school days together growing up in the little town of Tidioute, Pennsylvania, and swimming and fishing in the Allegheny River.

Chapter Three

A light frost dusted the ground the next morning. With a chill in the air, Samuel hustled to rekindle the fire so they could warm themselves and enjoy a cup of strong coffee. After feeding and watering the horses, they filled their canteens, smothered the flames with dirt, and headed toward Samuel's farm, still a day's ride away taking into account stopping occasionally. Samuel drove the wagon and Mark rode nearby so they could continue their conversation which turned to Indian relations and the progress made in peaceful negotiations over reservation boundaries in Kansas and adjoining states. "The Congress is considering options, but progress is slow." Samuel pointed out and Mark agreed.

"We had an incident with Indians coming to the farm trying to take a cow this winter. We ended up trading a first-year calf for three warm blankets. The calf would probably have starved had I kept it. The Indians were satisfied and we haven't seen them since, but they frightened Sarah terribly.

"So that's the one you traded." Mark shifted in his seat.

"Yes, this fall I hope to buy a few head to replace our losses if the grain fields produce."

"Passing through Missouri on our way to Kansas, we encountered our first horrifying experience with slavery. A white man claimed the boy he whipped had escaped and he owned the boy. The boy had a brand on his arm and the white man had papers to prove the brand belonged to him. The poor child was only about Jack's age, give or take a year or two, and from the scars on his back it wasn't the first time he'd seen the end of a whip. I just don't get it. Families owning black men, women and children. It's not right. They aren't property to be sold and traded. They're human beings for God's sake."

Mark nodded in agreement.

Samuel wasn't as knowledgeable as Mark on political issues. The controversy over slavery and how it tore the country apart with the North fighting against the practice and the South in favor dominated the conversation.

Then, they discussed whether Kansas would enter the Union as a free or a slave state supporting the Governing Union or the Rebel Confederates. Border skirmishes between Missouri and Kansas consumed the newspapers' headlines as the fights raged on.

"Sure glad we didn't settle near Atchison or Leavenworth. It's been a living hell there. Thankfully we haven't had any serious problems at the farm," Samuel said. It was good to catch up on the latest news. With Kansas a key state on slavery issues, Samuel would be sure to cast his vote.

"When I'm in town, talking political issues and slavery are off limits." Samuel straightened and stretched his back on the hard, wooden seat. "The tension in town is always high. That's why my family usually stays home and why we pretty much keep to ourselves."

He continued, "When you live in town, you either

own your own business, or you work for someone else. We wanted to work for ourselves and own our own land. We only venture to town when we need things. We live a day and a half ride away to keep our privacy. Mark, you lived growing up in town. Everyone knows your business. People are always coming and going. You're never sure who you can trust."

"That's the truth," Mark agreed. "But you must get mighty lonely at times, don't you? Especially the children and Sarah. They must yearn for the company of others."

"When we chose the land, we understood it meant sacrifices. We still honor the Lord's Day with prayer even though we don't go to church. In one way, we feel safer away from the activity of town.

"In other ways, it's affecting our children's education and social activities. Don't get me wrong, Mark. Sarah is a loving mother and a good teacher. Our children learn new things every day and they can care for themselves."

A mid-day pause broke their progress. The conversation turned to the weather and what the local newspaper predicted. "Says here a good year with ample rain." Samuel let out a sigh of relief.

Then with a slight grin he said, "Mark, Sarah and I worry about you."

"Oh?" Mark replied, and turned in his saddle toward his friend, the sun shining into his dark brown eyes.

"Well, you've never married. Are you ever going to settle down?"

Mark laughed. "You already married the prettiest girl from our hometown."

"Yes, and if I hadn't married her, you were next in line," Samuel boasted.

"I've been drifting for the last four years of my life, but I'm happy to say my search is over. Her name is Miss Katherine Weaver. She's pretty, but in a way different from Sarah. She's not petite. She's almost as tall as me, and she can lift a fifty pound sack of seed as easily as I can. I'm surprised how I feel when I'm around her. She is very caring, has a gentle touch and makes me feel loved and needed.

"Her father owns the hardware store in Heather Forks. It's about a week's ride from here. I worked at the store for a while. Katherine managed the counter and took care of the books. We got acquainted with each other while working together. She said she'd wait for me, but first some money would help. If only there were a gold mine hidden away somewhere with my name on its claim." Mark grinned from ear to ear. "Then we'd be set."

"I haven't asked her father for her hand in marriage yet, but I will when the time's right. There is a rancher in Nebraska who said he'd use me for cattle drives this year and my last boss paid well. I worked at a slaughterhouse this past winter, and the owner told me to come back anytime and he'd give me a job. Eventually Katherine and I want to buy our own place. Something large enough to raise children and keep a small herd of cattle."

"You're sure she's the one?" Samuel asked. "You're sure she can put up with you?"

"Yes, she's the one, and she can put up with me just fine. Shaking his head, Mark said, "Besides, with this scar on my face, I'm lucky she even wants me. And you know, Samuel, you're the only friend who could get away with asking me that. Then again, you're my only true friend." Mark lowered his brow.

"I told Katherine how I got the scar, about bluffing at the poker game and lying about having a gun under the table pointed at the other player. Remembering that broken whiskey bottle coming toward my face haunts me from time to time. It's still the closest I've come to dying." Mark's voice trailed off.

"I wanted to tell you about Katherine when we were all together, maybe sitting around the dinner table enjoying one of Sarah's fine meals."

"You still can. I'll act surprised. When can we meet her?"

"I've already told Katherine all about you and your family. She's anxious to meet you, but we'll have to wait until after we're married to make the trip. There's no way her father would let her come until then. My plan is to ask her to marry me next spring, after I have some extra money saved. Then we can buy land and start building a house."

"Building her a house will give you both a good start. You'll make a fine husband and a great father."

"We both want children, too. Hopefully a son one day. It must have been difficult for you when Sarah lost the baby, but I'm sure God will bless you again soon."

Samuel nodded. "Yes, and difficult for the children as well." He sighed. "Sarah lost one other baby, years ago. She carried the baby only a short while, but she was almost full term this time. She took it hard. She may be discouraged from trying again."

They rode in silence for a few minutes, then Samuel said, "Sarah always serves up supper when the pendulum clock her parents gave us for our wedding chimes five. We drug that clock clear from Pennsylvania and the time is still spot-on. The children love taking turns winding the key." *Hope they remembered to wind it today.*

"We better pick up the pace. We don't want to miss out on Sarah's cooking tonight." Thinking of food reminded Samuel about Sarah's project list. "You know, Sarah has a list of projects planned for us."

"She usually does. What's she want this year?"

"One thing is a shelf in the kitchen to hold her spice crocks. Oh, and she'd like a nightstand for the bedroom. Another on her list is to make the root cellar larger and add more shelves. We also have to rebuild the chicken coop that collapsed under a heavy snow in February. Luckily, we didn't lose any chickens. And I plan to clear more land this year to plant more corn, so we'll need to add onto the corncrib. We can use the lumber left from last year's corral project and salvage the wood from the old coop to build the new one."

"Sarah's shelf doesn't sound like it should take long. We should be able to work one into our busy schedule," Mark said. "It's always good to visit with you and your family, Samuel. It's at the top of my list to make this trip every year, but don't let me overstay my welcome."

"Mark, you've helped us a lot since we relocated out here and we really appreciate everything you've done. Send word when you want to get your house started. The whole family will come along to help. Oh, wait until you see the children. Jack's gotten tall. He told me Sarah measured him at five feet four. He's as slim as a stick, but he's strong. And Lydia has turned into quite the cook. My mouth waters thinking of her apple pie. She takes after her mother. Her smile is irresistible and when she sings, her voice is like an angel's. She'll make some man a good wife one day."

****

Samuel pulled the wagon into the yard and Sarah poked her head out the door. "Hurry! Supper is ready." The men tended the horses and washed up before entering the house.

At the door, Mark took off his hat and ran his fingers through his hair.

"You go first. They see me all the time." Samuel stepped back.

Mark called out, "Sure smells good in here!"

"Uncle Mark, you made it." Jack lunged forward, shaking his hand.

Lydia approached next. "Ma just said we were going to eat without you if you didn't get here soon."

Mark bent over, hugged Lydia and kissed the top of her head.

"Eat without us? You wouldn't do that would you, Sarah?" Mark leaned over and kissed Sarah on her cheek.

Sarah blushed. "How are you, Mark? It's so good to have you with us."

"I'm fine and I'm hungry. Your fried chicken sure smells good. Did Lydia help?" Mark turned and gave Lydia a wink.

"Yup. Hope you like it, Uncle Mark. We butchered two chickens, special for tonight. We'll have enough for carcass soup, too," Lydia suggested. "And oh, wait till you try my apple pie. There isn't a dried apple left in the root cellar because we used every last one.

"Sounds delicious. I'll be sure to leave room for dessert." Mark hung his hat and coat on a hook by the door, then picked up Lydia, twirling her twice, before setting her back down. "My, you and Jack have both grown since last year."

Sarah made a sweeping motion with her arms. "Now everyone to the table before the food gets cold."

Samuel and Sarah's gazes met while Mark talked with the children. Samuel walked over to his wife, slipped his arms around her waist, and quickly kissed the back of her neck. "You look beautiful, dear," he whispered. Sarah accepted his attention and Samuel took this as a good sign. "Let me help you carry the food to the table."

Sarah wore a freshly-pressed, blue flowered dress with her hair neatly combed. The table was set with the company linens and the children dressed in their best clothes in honor of the occasion.

All through supper, Jack and Lydia sat wide-eyed, their food growing cold as Mark told of his escapades over the past year.

"Lydia, your pie is absolutely delicious. Best I've eaten in a long while," Mark said after taking his first bite.

Lydia's eyes lit up and her smile showed off her dimples. "Glad you like it, Uncle Mark."

Samuel also commented, "This is the best apple pie you've made since the last one we ate, sweetheart."

Again, Lydia's dimples appeared and she said, "Oh Pa, you always like pie. It doesn't matter what kind of pie, it's always your favorite."

When the last fork rested on the plate, the children jumped up to clear the dishes, but Sarah told them to sit back down. She'd do the dishes as Mark told about his cattle drive stories that always seemed to end up in sticky situations.

"My right eye turned black and blue for days after one scuffle, but the other guy's nose was broken and a tooth was gone. Only escaped the sheriff by a few minutes," Mark said concluding another adventurous tale.

When Mark started to talk about the last ranch where he worked as a cowhand, the children wanted details, but Sarah interrupted. "Let's save a few stories for another night. Come on children, it's near your bedtime. Go wash up."

"But Ma, do we have to? One more story, please, Ma," Jack said.

Lydia chimed in, "It wouldn't be polite to go to bed when Uncle Mark has more stories to tell."

"Go get washed up now." Samuel's voice interjected. "Mark will always have more stories to share and he will be here a few weeks, so let's keep some for another night."

The children obeyed and trudged off. Ready for bed, they said their goodnights and headed for the loft where Sarah joined them for prayers.

Back at the table, Sarah stood behind Samuel, leaned down to kiss his cheek, and said, "Don't you two stay up all night. Mark, you're in Jack's bed as usual. He fixed himself a pallet out of quilts and blankets on the floor. Don't worry, he loves it when you come to stay and doesn't mind this arrangement at all." Then she disappeared into their bedroom, leaving the men to catch up on news and reminisce about their early pre-Sarah years back in Pennsylvania before turning in for the night.

****

Immediately after breakfast the next morning, Samuel and Mark started building the chicken coop.

"A perfect day for an outdoor project," Samuel said, as he gathered tools and headed toward the east end of the barn. The new coop would be bigger and have an earthen floor because a wooden one was too costly. Samuel had already set the posts for the walls. After tamping down the ground around the posts, the measuring, cutting, and hammering began.

The two men worked side by side all day with Jack assisting when his chores were done. The boards from the old structure were salvaged to make the coop's board and batten walls and quickly nailed into place.

After a break mid-day, they returned to work installing the nesting boxes and a bench beneath the glass-paned window. This time Samuel would make a better door with a secure latch. The family depended too heavily on the eggs and the meat to lose any more chickens.

They were clearing the work area for the day when Sarah called them for supper.

"It'll take us at least the rest of tomorrow to tackle the coop roof and door. Then our plan is to extend the corncrib. Afterward, we'll start on your list, Sarah," Samuel said. He gave her a wink as he and Mark walked outside to enjoy the cigars Mark bought in town, a special indulgence after a hard day's work.

That evening, in bed, Samuel quietly told Sarah about Miss Katherine Weaver. "Great news. You won't believe it, sweetheart, but Mark is finally ready to settle down, get married, and raise a family. He thinks he finally found the right gal."

Sarah couldn't believe her ears.

"Her name is Katherine Weaver and she lives in Missouri. He's going to tell us about her sometime, so act surprised when he does, all right?"

"Of course, dear," Sarah agreed, then asked, "Do you really think Mark will settle down, or does he enjoy the cattle drives, moving from place to place and telling tales of his adventures too much to tie himself to one woman?"

"I don't know, sweetheart. You can ask him yourself." Samuel gave Sarah a goodnight kiss before he blew out the lamp and settled to sleep.

****

The next morning, Jack did the barn chores as the men finished the roof and made the new door.

By late afternoon, the coop was almost complete. The only thing left was to frame out and hang the door.

Samuel read Sarah's list aloud, " 'a shelf in the kitchen to hold my spice crocks, a nightstand for the bedroom, and expand the root cellar lined with shelves.' There's still time to get the kitchen shelf started today."

"My room could really use a shelf with pegs to hang up clothes," Jack said. "The shelf would be the perfect place for my rock collection."

"Sure, Jack. There'll be enough scrap lumber for you to build one."

"Great. I'll hang it at the foot of bed."

The next day, after constructing and installing Sarah's shelf, the two men hung the door for the coop, introduced the chickens to their new home, and started on the five-foot corncrib extension. Samuel figured the project would take at least two days.

After dinner, Mark gave the children the two bags of candy he brought from town. Delighted with their surprises, they sat and indulged themselves with the unexpected sweets.

Samuel invited Mark to take a ride out to the fields so he could show him the additional land he intended to cultivate.

The two men discussed at length what crops Samuel should plant to avert another winter disaster.

"How about barley and rye grass?" Mark asked.

The four-acre clover field made exceptional pasture for spring and summer grazing and kept the cattle close to the farm. Even though they weren't fenced, the cows never roamed too far from the pasture and the stream. The corn, hay and oats fed the herd, milk cow, horses, and chickens. The feed would be stored in the old structure built their first year as a shelter and now used as the storage shed.

"The barley and rye grass could be used as feed and Sarah could even cook the barley in soups and stews," Mark said.

"All this sounds very encouraging, but we're not out of the woods yet," Samuel opined. "If this growing season is as hard on crops as last year, no matter how many acres we plant, there still won't be enough feed for the animals or any left to sell to pay down my store bills."

"Farming is a hard life," Mark replied, "but you've known that from the start. Look how far you've come in four years. Be proud of your successes, Samuel, and keep working toward your dream. Someday you'll turn this place into a self-sufficient farm."

****

To expand the root cellar located behind the house, the men first carried the crocks and produce stored inside to the storage shed. Jack, eager to help, soon decided schoolwork was easier.

Mark wiped the sweat from his forehead. "Jack had the right idea, schoolwork sounds much better. You think he needs any help?"

Samuel laughed out loud and shook his head. "If you recall, you weren't all that good in school."

"No, the schoolwork wasn't the problem. Sitting beside Claire Jenkins was the problem. Fishing, hunting or any place was better than school. Why did we always have to sit in alphabetical order?"

They both chuckled.

One shovelful at a time, they entered and exited the cramped space as the underground room expanded until Sarah agreed it was large enough. The two men installed the support beams and built sturdy shelves with tree logs and the few pieces of leftover lumber.

More lumber would be needed to finish the project, but while Samuel had Mark's help, they would use every scrap of wood on hand. A small stash of 'good wood', as Samuel called it, he saved to make Sarah a special piece of furniture someday. Now he selected a few pieces to make the night stand she requested.

With the larger projects out of the way, the two men anticipated their hunting trip.

Samuel explained his plans to Sarah. "A few men in town were talking about Blue Rapids and how the hunting was good there this year. We could bring home fresh meat for the Easter and Thanksgiving Day table. Do you mind if we go? We'd only be gone three or four days."

Sarah smiled and replied, "Some fresh venison sure would help stretch meals. Most of the beef we made into jerky or brined. A deer or two would last a while. Don't worry about being away. Since Mark arrived, schoolwork has lagged. The children can catch up on reading and arithmetic."

Jack, eager to go along, said, "Twelve is old enough to go on an overnight hunt isn't it, Father?"

"Yes, but not this time, son. We'll take you along on a day hunt while Uncle Mark is here. Perhaps in a few weeks for a turkey. Uncle Mark plans on staying for Easter and the following week is Thanksgiving. We'll have time for a turkey hunt. How's that sound?"

"All right I guess." Jack scuffed his foot under the table.

Samuel was proud of the work accomplished since Mark's arrival and was ready for the hunting trip with his good friend the next morning.

****

"Only four days," Samuel told Sarah as he stole a hug and good-bye kiss, gratefully accepting the bundle of food she packed. He was glad to see her back to her old self. He and the children missed her during her time of grief. Mark's visit turned into a blessing for the entire family.

Samuel filled his canteen at the well and walked to the barn where he found his children helping Mark pack his saddlebags. Samuel kissed each child. "Take care of your mother," he said as he swung up onto the saddle. Button, his horse, was ready to leave.

Mark mounted Ruby and followed Samuel out of the barn.

The children joined Sarah by the well.

"Pa, do you mind if I use your tools to work on my shelf? I want to have mine finished by the time you return."

"All right, Jack, but please be careful."

Heading for the barn, Jack called out, "This project might take me a while to finish, Ma."

Sarah called after him, "Chores first and then your shelf."

Everyone waved good-bye.

"Fresh venison sure will taste good!" Jack shouted as the men rode off.

Samuel looked over his shoulder and waved.

****

The two friends rode out with the heat of the sun warming their faces. Still on Samuel's property, they shot two rabbits which they skinned and salted.

"At least we have supper covered." Samuel chuckled.

About a mile from the farm, at the farthest point of his property, Samuel stopped before crossing the creek. His family was fortunate to have this little stream which ran year-round through the property. "Someday I'd like to build a bridge here," he told Mark. He continued, "This is the very spot where Sarah's Brother, Richard, got shot defending his land rights from claim jumpers. Did I ever tell you what happened that day?"

"No, Samuel, tell me."

"Well, Richard and I were coming back from town with a load of lumber and supplies to finish building the cabin. The day was hot and we couldn't wait to get back to the house for a glass of cool mint tea. Without Richard's contributions of materials, his strength, and his carpentry skills, the house wouldn't be built as fine."

Samuel and Mark got off their horses and stood at the creek bank. Staring down into the creek, red-stained water was all Samuel could see no matter the time of day or season. He shook his head and recalled the fateful events to Mark.

"Richard drove the wagon and when we got closer to the creek, four figures on the other side appeared to be piling creek rocks to make a corner marker staking claim to what was actually Richard's property. A fifth person drove a wagon laden with rocks dug from the creek bed, kegs of nails, a couple of barrels, and some lumber.

"Richard called across the creek, 'Who's in charge here?'

"The men paid no attention. Richard eased the horses and wagon into the creek where the splashing finally got the men's attention. Without warning, a boy in the other wagon drew his pistol and shot Richard who slumped in the seat next to me and fell forward into the creek.

"With my hands raised, I looked down at Richard in the water. He floated, face down, with blood pooling around him. The red stain slowly followed the current of the water downstream.

"I yelled, 'Don't shoot' and leapt into the creek to get to Richard. The other men helped lift him onto the shore. Richard coughed a few times, looked up at me and said, 'Help me, Samuel,' and then lost consciousness. I couldn't believe what had just happened. The shot was so sudden and such a shock. How could I tell Sarah? What would I say to our family?

"As they lifted Richard into the back of our wagon, making room for him among the lumber and building supplies, the older man who turned out to be the father of the four young men was very upset and shaken. He sputtered, 'A big misunderstanding. This was all a big misunderstanding.'

"He explained they understood the land was available. Their family encountered problems on their journey west with others stealing from them. The boy who shot Richard had a horse stolen from him, one he raised from a colt. These events made him edgy toward strangers.

"The boy cried out. 'It's my fault. I'm sorry, I'm sorry. You surprised me. I didn't mean to hurt anyone. Please don't send me to jail.'

"I told them I'd tell the sheriff the incident was an accident...it truly was, but it didn't make my acceptance of the situation any easier.

"The father stuffed a coin pouch into my shirt pocket. 'Here, take this. It's all we have. Use it for medicine.'

"His money wouldn't have made a difference to poor Richard. I threw the pouch on the ground and told them, 'Take your money and get out of here. Get out fast before I change my mind.'

"What was done was done. Richard was bleeding heavily. A decision had to be made and quickly. I wasn't sure Richard would last a day to get him to the doctor in Dead Flats. The bullet appeared to have gone clear through his chest. So I took him home to Sarah. Richard lay unconscious in blood soaked clothes when we arrived at the farm. Jack and Sarah ran out when they heard the wagon pull in. They helped carry

Richard to bed. He lost so much blood. Only a miracle could save him.

"Sarah immediately made poultices and placed them on the wound. Richard weak and very pale would sometimes open his eyes as he drifted in and out of consciousness. Sarah tended his wound day and night, resting only short periods when we insisted.

"Two days passed and sadly Richard slipped away during the early hours as Sarah sat holding his hand, praying for a miracle. With heavy hearts, we buried Richard under the old elm tree on the hill near the house.

"He was a good man and a good friend," Samuel said as he hung his head.

"Yes, Richard was a good man. I remember him from school. You never shared this with me before," Mark said. "It must have been hard on the family."

"Yes, very difficult especially for Sarah and the children. That's why I hated leaving Sarah alone this morning after all she's endured the past few years. She lost Richard and now the baby." Samuel said a silent prayer for Sarah and added, *Please let Mark's presence help the healing process for Sarah and the children. Our recent loss took its toll on everyone.*

"This spot by the creek stirs up memories every trip," Samuel said as he mounted Button and urged the horse forward.

****

In the afternoon, Samuel shouldered his rifle at a deer grazing on tender grass about forty paces away, but the deer suddenly ducked into taller grass and he never got off the shot. In the late afternoon they spotted a flock of turkeys combing a field of grass. Both men took aim and two birds lay waiting for them as they walked to claim their rewards. Sarah would be pleased. Later at their campsite, Mark dressed out the birds and salted them while Samuel built a fire, roasted the rabbits, and shoved potatoes into the embers.

Disappointed he didn't have more to offer, Samuel joked, "A rabbit and a potato will have to do for supper tonight."

Chapter Four

After a few hours in the saddle the next morning, Samuel and Mark still hadn't seen a deer or any wild game. Taking a short break for a drink of water and a piece of jerky, the two men looked out over the flat Kansas plains.

Samuel started the conversation, "Mark, you never told Sarah and the children about Miss Katherine."

"You never gave me a chance, old friend, working me from sun-up to sun-down. But don't worry, there'll be time when we get back." Then Mark reminisced, "Hey, remember the day in the sixth grade when we skipped school and took off hunting behind Mr. Hain's farm? We both brought home squirrels that day. Talk about a fine day's hunt. We were good with shotguns when we were young but doubt we could do it now." Mark took a long swig from his canteen and set it on a rock.

"My sack had six squirrels and yours only four." Samuel chuckled.

"Your memory's going, my friend. My sack had seven and yours only five," Mark reminded him.

"Well, maybe you're right." Samuel sighed. "We best be moving along. We haven't put any food on the table yet today."

The men headed northeast toward Blue Rapids looking for wildlife and enjoying the fresh smell of spring in the air.

They'd ridden a couple of miles when Mark looked down and his canteen was missing from its usual spot next to his leather scabbard. "Hey, stop," Mark called up to Samuel. "My canteen is missing. Must be back at our last stop. I hate to waste the time but can't really manage without it. Why don't you stay close to the path and keep hunting? It won't take me long to go fetch my canteen and catch up with you."

"Okay. There're woods up ahead and I'll wait for you there. Maybe something will be out feeding."

Mark nodded, took off his hat to run his fingers through his long brown hair, waved and headed back at a good pace the way they came.

Samuel waited until Mark was down the road a piece then headed for the woods. Farther down the road and over a knoll, a stagecoach had stopped alongside the trail. It tilted to one side and two men were using a crowbar and a board trying to lift the coach while a young boy attempted to slide a wheel into position.

The sun warmed Samuel's back as he nudged his horse into a gallop and headed in their direction to give a hand. The two men wiped their brow before attempting to position the wheel again. He yelled out, "Hold on a second if you fellows want a hand."

Startled by the stranger's voice, the men looked up and Samuel jumped off his horse and ran to their aid. He grabbed a corner of the wagon and settled his shoulder against the carriage.

The driver said, "I'll count to three. You all take a deep breath and lift while the boy tries again."

The boy nodded and the driver counted, "One. Two. Three."

Each man breathed deep and lifted with all his might. The boy struggled but managed to slide the wheel into place and the men let out a collective sigh of relief. Glancing at the boy, Samuel noticed a large birthmark on his neck just below his ear.

"Thanks for your help, young fella. We appreciate you stopping. Where're you heading?" the driver asked, wiping his hands on his pants as he checked to make sure the wheel was secured.

"A friend's waiting for me and we're headed to Blue Rapids to hunt. We heard there's deer in the area and we're looking to put some food away before planting the fields."

The other man was well dressed. He and the boy appeared to be father and son. Each shared the same high forehead and piercing blue eyes. They were wiping their hands in the grass trying to clean off the grease.

"Where's the stage headed?" Samuel asked over his shoulder as he walked to his horse.

"We're on our way to Marysville. After all this, we'll be a little late."

Mounting Button, Samuel caught a glimpse of two men on horseback riding toward them at a gallop. They must have been hiding in the small copse of trees up the trail.

"Looks like trouble," Samuel shouted to the driver.

The father yelled to his son, "Billy, get in the coach. Crouch down on the floor and stay there!" The boy did as he was told.

The driver jumped up onto the seat and grabbed the reins of the four-horse team. "They're after the payroll!" he shouted.

37

"Payroll! But you don't have anyone riding shotgun." Samuel yelled. A glance under the driver's seat revealed a padlocked cashbox.

"We hoped to get through if we acted like we weren't carrying. Its payroll money," the driver said, "and those men probably don't care if they have to kill to get it.

The first shot rang out, hitting the boy's father who crumpled to his knees, then fell to the ground, dead. Samuel heard the boy scream, 'Father!' Samuel instinctively shouldered his rifle and shot back.

Samuel yelled to the boy, "Stay in the coach. Get down!" They were an easy target standing still, so he shouted to the driver, "Take off! Hurry! We'll come back for the body if we get out of this alive."

The driver whipped the reins and urged the horses who lunged forward, pulling the coach back onto the trail. More gunfire rang out. A bullet zinged past barely missing Samuel's head, so close he heard the bullet streak by. He fired repeatedly at the two men now rapidly closing the distance to the stagecoach. One outlaw fell to the ground and Samuel continued shooting until his rifle was empty. He quickly holstered the rifle and drew his revolver. Using his arm as a rest, he took aim and fired carefully. The second outlaw fell from his horse and lay dead on the trail. Where there only two men or possibly more coming?

Samuel, pulled back on Button's reins, keeping an eye peeled for others. He had killed two men. He never shot anything before he didn't plan on eating. Now two men lay dead by his hand. Surging adrenaline made everything a blur. He stopped and waited until the stagecoach driver slowed the raging horses to a gradual stop.

Riding to the coach, Samuel's mind floated as though he was in slow motion. His ears rang from the shooting. Seeing nobody else coming, he unlatched the stagecoach door. The boy was still crouched on the floor, eyes filled with tears and shaking.

"It's all right. It's over," he told the boy. "No more shooting."

The driver was clutching his arm. "You've been hit!" Samuel yelled. He told the boy, "Jump up on the seat and help the driver."

Seeing the blood, the boy quickly took out his bandana and tied it as tight as he could to slow the bleeding. "My father was dead from the first shot," the boy said, still shaking.

"Thanks for everything!" The driver yelled to Samuel. "We'll go back and pick up the boy's father and the other bodies and get their horses as well. There's bound to be a reward for saving the payroll, Mister.

The driver's words barely registered with Samuel. Something warm ran down his neck at his collar. He touched the wound. He'd been hit in the neck on the left side. He applied pressure firmly to slow the bleeding, but blood soaked his hand. Struggling to stay upright in the saddle, he yelled to the driver, "You tell the sheriff the way this all happened so our stories match. In a few weeks I'll come pick up the reward and the bounty on those outlaws. Sorry about your father, son, but I have to leave."

"I'll make sure the sheriff gets the whole story. You deserve that reward, young fella. You saved our lives." Then the driver called out, "Hey, what's your name?", but Samuel was out of earshot and didn't look back.

After a few miles or so, Samuel could barely hold the reins and slowed to a stop. Excruciating pain radiated through his head and body as he slowly slid from Button to his knees and then fell forward, face down onto the ground. Blood seeped through his fingers as he cupped his hand to his neck with what little energy he had left. Did Mark hear the gunfight? Was he on his way to help?

Chapter Five

Mark retrieved his canteen and headed in the direction he and Samuel last parted. A gunshot rang out, he kicked Ruby into a gallop. *Great, maybe Samuel got a deer.* Then, another shot. *Was that a rifle or a pistol?* Then a barrage of fire from two, maybe three guns. Holding tight to the reins, Mark urged Ruby on. *Samuel's in trouble.* As he rode frantic to find his friend, sweat beaded on his forehead.

Soon he spotted Samuel's horse ahead standing beside a crumpled form on the ground. *No, it can't be. Please, God, don't let that be Samuel.* Drawing closer, a man's body lay in a fetal position with a blood soaked shirt and coat and a hand clutching his neck. Mark gasped, "Samuel, no, not Samuel."

Ruby skidded to a stop and Mark leapt from the saddle and knelt at Samuel's side. He looked into his friend's pain-filled eyes. "Let me see," he said, fearing the worse.

Samuel removed his hand for a second and then grasped his neck again, unable to staunch the flow of blood that spewed from between his fingers.

"You'll be all right," Mark whispered. He ripped off his shirtsleeve to plug and wrap the wound, then watched helplessly as the improvised bandage did nothing to stop the bleeding.

Samuel coughed a weak laugh and shivered, sweat

41

beading on his pale cheeks and forehead. "You never were a good liar."

"Lie? Me? Never." Mark tried to smile.

As Mark got up to fetch his bedroll to cover his dying friend, Samuel said, "Don't leave me."

With Samuel propped against him, Mark applied more pressure to the wound and asked, "What happened?"

"Two men," Samuel whispered, "two men held up the stage. They killed Billy's father. Shot the driver in the arm. Remember this," Samuel insisted, "so you can collect the reward."

"What reward?"

"Tell the sheriff, and the reward money will pay off my debts," Samuel wheezed, "so Sarah can keep the farm." Samuel winced and groaned. His eyes welled with tears.

"Take it easy. You need to rest." Mark applied more pressure.

"A dark birthmark under his ear." Samuel started to shake.

"Who?" Mark asked.

"Billy," Samuel panted.

Mark hugged Samuel close to him. "Oh, Samuel, why you? That damn canteen. I should be laying here, not you. Why, God? Why Samuel?" Mark repositioned his hand on the wound that would not be staunched.

"Collect the reward. Promise. Sarah needs the money."

Mark nodded.

Samuel closed his eyes for a moment and then murmured, "Blood money, she'd call it." His body twitched uncontrollably. "Don't tell her I killed two men. No violence."

"No violence," Mark repeated. "She knows you would never kill anyone, but this was different. You were defending yourself. "Are you sure you don't want me to tell her?"

Samuel nodded.

"Then she'll never know." Mark assured him.

"Promise."

"Yes, I promise. She'll never learn the truth about the robbery or the killing."

Samuel gasped and struggled to open his eyes one last time. He said in a low whisper, "One kiss. Sarah. My children."

Mark held Samuel not wanting to let go but helpless as his mortally wounded friend's life slowly ebbed.

"Please take care of them."

Mark replied quickly, time was of the essence, "Yes, Samuel. Don't worry. I'll take care of them."

Eyes closed, seemingly at peace after hearing Mark's promise. Samuel whispered, "I love her," as he took his last breath on earth and his body fell limp and lifeless.

****

Cradling his lifelong friend in his arms, he hesitated, wishing this were a dream. *Why Samuel? He had so much to live for.* Torn between remembering old times and the questions that crowded his mind, Mark thrashed thoughts back and forth, then sat in shock as the sun became a brilliant sliver on the horizon.

Darkness would soon be on them. Shaking himself free from these churning thoughts, he quickly wrapped his friend in the bedroll blanket and struggled to lift

Samuel's lifeless body onto Button. Getting back to the farm was foremost in his mind, but close on its heels was the burning question…what in God's name was he going to tell Sarah?

****

Marysville sheriff, Reed Kurtz paced between his desk and the rifle cabinet, as sweat beaded on his brow. *Should I gather a posse? It's not like the stage to be this late and it's carrying a cash box…payroll money.* Just then the sound of the four-horse team thundered down the main street of town. *I'll skin his hide if he doesn't have a good excuse.* Finally breathing a sigh of relief, Kurtz grabbed his rifle and ran to meet the coach. Was the money safe? What had happened?

"Sheriff Kurtz, an attempted robbery!" Old Buck, the driver called out while pulling back on the reins. Billy, sitting beside him, braced for the end of the wild ride. "They didn't get it, though!" Buck shouted as the stagecoach rolled to a stop in front of the saloon. Folks gathered in excitement.

"We'd thrown a wheel and this man who looked like a farmer stopped and offered to help. Then out of nowhere rode two riders with guns a-blazing. Their first shot killed this boy's father. The stranger said to charge them. We were sitting targets if we hadn't."

Buck jumped down as he continued to relay his adventure, "I took the reins, and we headed the stage straight at them. That farmer shot them both. I told him he could collect a reward for saving the payroll money. The farmer figured the outlaws had a bounty on them and said he'd collect that reward too. He deserves it. Every penny of it, if you ask me," Buck said. "He definitely had a firm hand shake. A bounty hunter wouldn't have let those outlaws out of his sight. The farmer looked directly at the cashbox. His eyes widened, but he never made a move for it. Didn't get his name 'cause things happened too fast, but he told me to tell you he'd be in to collect the reward. He told me to tell you what happened."

"I'll need you to swear out a deposition these facts are true. Come over to the office once your wound is tended to and you can fill in all the details." Sheriff Kurtz scratched his chin.

Buck opened the door to reveal the bodies of Billy's father and the two outlaws, as the young boy jumped down from the stage.

"The man who saved us said he had to go find his friend. Here are the two robbers who tried to do us in, Sheriff," Buck said, pointing, "These here are the two outlaws."

"Deputies," Sheriff Kurtz called, "come pull these men out of the coach, then carry the cash box to the bank. And one of you go fetch the doc to see to Buck's arm."

Buck took off his hat and dusted it, hitting it across his knee a few times. "But there's worse news, Sheriff. This man"—he pointed down at the boy's dead father—"this man and his son were passengers from Kansas City. His name's Jacob Henry. He was out in the open when the riders began firing and was killed by one of the first shots fired. Sad thing though, his son, who told me his name is Billy," the driver said pointing to the boy, "saw it happen."

Motioning to the deputies who were back from the bank, the sheriff said, "C'mon, help me get these three to the undertaker." Then the sheriff abruptly motioned for them to stop. "Second thought let's see if they got any money first."

"Gosh, Sheriff, we wanted to get to town as quick as possible, so we loaded them in the coach and took off hoping there weren't more outlaws waiting for us. I never checked their pockets." Buck rubbed his chin.

Before Buck left with the doctor to have his wound treated, he took Kurtz aside and said, "The boy and I talked some on the ride in. Don't think he has any other family. The boy's your problem now, Sheriff."

"Make sure you see me when you're done at the doc's. I want some more details about this so called farmer who saved you. If he's comin' for the reward I'll have to identify him," Kurtz said and looked at the boy.

Billy, tears in his eyes, knelt at his father's still form. He unhooked his father's pocket watch and slipped it into his own pocket. Next, he removed his father's coin pouch and put it in his other pocket.

Sheriff Kurtz said gruffly, "Sorry for your loss, son." He patted the boy on the shoulder and said, "Come with me."

Chapter Six

We were just telling tales on each other this morning and now you're gone, Samuel. You may not blame me for your death, but I blame myself. I should have been there with you. I've known you for as long as I can remember. You're my best friend. We'd go swimming in the river, catch frogs, fishing, hunting, school; we even loved the same woman once. How could you just up and die on me? By the time I got to you, you'd already lost too much blood. My God Samuel, what will I do without you? What will Sarah and the children do without you?

Mark held the reins to lead Samuel's horse with the body tied to it. The going was slow traveling by moonlight, giving him more time to think than he really wanted. Sarah and the children were on his mind. Their world would soon tumble down around them, but he couldn't let that happen. He needed to be there for them as Samuel had asked.

Although Samuel was a hero in Mark's eyes, he pondered how he could explain the reward money and the bounty without telling Sarah the truth. Two lies. It would take two lies, one about Samuel's death and another about the money.

Samuel wanted something good to come from his death, Mark mused. *Could collecting the reward be pulled off without getting caught? What if I mix up facts when I'm talking to the sheriff? Maybe the stagecoach driver already claimed the money for himself? Does the possible outcome outweigh the risk? I can't let down my best friend and his family.*

Mark's mind shifted to the orphaned boy, Billy. *The poor child's father was killed. The boy's family suffered a loss too. There was a birthmark on his neck. Details. That's what Samuel told me. Remember the details.*

Dawn cast its shadows and although Mark was bone weary, he kept riding. Soon the cluster of trees along the creek where he and Samuel crossed two days before were in view. The farm was close now, about two miles away.

He stopped to let the horses drink and to eat his last piece of jerky as he nervously paced, pondering what to tell Sarah. Unbidden, an image of Miss Katherine Weaver awaiting his return flashed before his eyes, but he rejected it. He needed to focus. He needed to come up with a story, really a lie that would honor his promise to Samuel and at the same time be a story Sarah wouldn't question.

Most important, he needed to convince Sarah to let him stay on and help plant the crops. Mark hated to lie, but Samuel made him promise. Sarah would never learn the truth even though the circumstances were self-defense. Mark's promise to Samuel was one promise to his best friend he intended to keep no matter what. Sarah and the children needed him.

Mark let the horses nibble at the grass along the bank as he sat on a downed tree limb trying to piece together a believable story.

What if Indians ambushed us? Samuel mentioned

an incident with Indians. Maybe they could be after meat and tried to take a deer we shot. During the shooting, maybe Samuel got hit? Then the Indians took Samuel's horse with the deer tied to it and rode off. Indians needed meat too. The winter took its toll on everyone. But would they go so far as to kill for food?

After trying to make it work, Mark rejected this idea. *No, if Indians killed Samuel, Sarah would want the sheriff to investigate. The story must seem like an accident that took Samuel's life...no violence.*

What if a rattlesnake spooked Samuel's horse? No, not warm enough for snakes just yet. How about if Button stumbled in a prairie dog hole and threw Samuel? Yes, that could happen. But then how could they keep Button knowing he caused Samuel's death?

We were on a hunting trip, so that fact needs worked into the story. How about this? We shot a deer, had field dressed it and were packing the meat on Samuel's horse. The coyotes we passed a few miles back heard the shots and rushed in from behind looking for a free meal. Samuel's horse must have smelled them. One growled before the pack charged in for the gut pile. Button bucked and kicked, then ran off. Samuel said, 'Darn, now I have to go chase down Button.' Then, Samuel trips and falls backward, landing hard and hitting his head on a patch of rocks. He tells me he's in pain as he tries to sit up. When he lifted his head, blood gushed from a bad wound on his neck. We couldn't stop the bleeding. By this time the coyotes ran off following Button's scent. This is good. No one is to blame. It just happens.

Mark ran the story through his head a few more times working out the details. *Shoot deer, coyotes come for gut pile, Button rears up, kicks, and runs off with the deer tied to his saddle. Samuel is annoyed he has to chase after Button, trips and falls backward hitting his head on sharp rocks. Bleeding won't stop, coyotes follow Button. But, what about losing the horse? We'll need Button for plowing. I'll have to let him go and hope he finds his way home in a day or two. This is the story.* Mark, both exhausted and relieved prayed, *Lord, forgive me for lying, but please let Sarah believe me.*

At the creek bank, Mark untied Samuel's body and lifted him from his horse. He washed the dried blood from his friends face and neck so Sarah wouldn't have to see it. Then he changed Samuel's shirt and used his own bedroll to wrap Samuel. Quickly he dug a hole near the creek, buried all of Samuel's bloody belongings and covered them with dirt and brush. The hole was deep enough to keep away animals. He'd dig a deeper one when time permitted. With difficulty, Mark lifted Samuel's body up onto his own horse, Ruby.

Mark turned Button loose after cinching the saddle and tying the reins so they wouldn't get caught in brush. Mark wanted the horse to feed a while and not follow immediately. He would also mention he saw Indians on his return. Sarah's caution level would rise and she'd worry about the Indians, but that might help convince her to let Mark stay until the crops were in.

Pausing before leaving the creek, he patted the blanket covering Samuel and said aloud, "I promised I'd watch over Sarah and the children and use the reward money to pay off your debts. I aim to uphold my promise, old friend. I'll take care of them."

Back on the path to the farm, Mark rehearsed his story several times to make it sound convincing.

Approaching the farm, he dismounted behind the barn and walked beside Samuel's body to keep it from being seen. This way he could tell Sarah what happened when they were alone. The news would break her heart and devastate the children.

His plan was good, but Lydia caught him as he turned the corner. Mark hurried toward the barn, but she called out. "Uncle Mark, you're back early. Ma wasn't expecting you back so soon. She'll be surprised to see you."

Mark took a step back to conceal Samuel's body and put up his palm, halting her. "Lydia, please, stop right there. I need you to fetch your mother and then you and Jack need to wait in the house until one of us comes for you. Hurry now. Tell her I need to see her in the barn."

Obeying the urgency in Mark's voice, Lydia ran to the house yelling, "Ma! Ma, come quick! Uncle Mark is back!"

Sarah heard her daughter's voice and opened the door as Lydia called, "Uncle Mark wants to see you in the barn, but he sent me to the house. He said Jack and I have to stay here until you come for us. Can't I come with you, Ma? Please."

"If Mark sent you to the house, there is a good reason. You go inside and stay there with Jack. I'll be in shortly." Sarah ran into the barn and found Mark standing by Ruby with the limp form draped over the horse's back. She stopped and fell to her knees her whole body shaking. "Please tell me that isn't Samuel," she said in a low cry. "Please, Mark, please tell me that isn't my beloved Samuel."

Mark, with tears in his eyes, looked at Sarah. With

everything she had endured he hated to tell her, yet she needed to know. "Yes, Sarah, I'm so sorry. It's as you fear, it's Samuel." It broke his heart to lie to Sarah and it took all the willpower he could muster not to tell the truth, but that's what Samuel wanted. Mark lied to keep his promise.

****

Sarah rose unsteadily and stumbled forward to stand beside her husband. She placed her arms across the blanket and rested her face on his lifeless form. She suddenly pulled furiously at the blanket trying to expose Samuel's face, not wanting to believe Mark until she looked for herself. "Oh, no," she sobbed seeing Samuel's face with his eye's closed. Then she discovered the puncture wound to his neck. "What happened? You must tell me what happened." Tears streamed down her cheeks, as she held tight to her husband's breathless body. "Tell me Mark. No matter how painful to hear, I must know the truth. What happened?" Sarah's tone demanded an answer.

"We were hunting on our way to Blue Rapids and Samuel shot a deer. We just finished tying the deer on Button when coyotes appeared. The pack must have heard the shot and gathered to see if there was a gut pile for them."

"Coyotes?" She sobbed.

"Button whinnied and made a fuss. I turned in time to see him buck hard and run off. Samuel even joked, 'Button never did like coyotes. Now we'll have to go chase him down.' Then the coyotes took off after Button as we emptied our pistols at them, but two got away. Next thing I knew, Samuel tripped, fell backward, and hit the ground hard, real hard. The fall seemed to knock the wind out of him and his head struck an outcrop of sharp rocks and his neck was bleeding. When he finally came around, he complained his back and neck hurt. When he tried to lift his head, blood gushed from his wound. I did everything I could, but it wouldn't stop bleeding. Samuel couldn't breathe and said every part of his body ached. With all the blood lost, he couldn't last long. I was with him every minute, Sarah, right up to the end."

"Is this a dream? It has to be a dream," Sarah said through her tears. "My Samuel can't be gone. What will we do without him? How will we manage? The children. My poor children have lost their father. First Richard, then Baby Walter, and now Samuel. How is this possible? How will we manage the farm?" Again, she wrapped herself around Samuel's body.

Her heart heavy with sadness, realization slowly dawned on her, she and the children were now alone. Her true love was gone. "What will we do?" she asked again. "How can the children and I ever survive without Samuel?"

Mark gently touched her on the shoulder.

Sarah put her hand on Mark's arm. "Thank God you're here, Mark. And thank God you were with Samuel so he didn't die alone." Then the blood on Mark's shirtsleeves caught her attention.

"He died in my arms, Sarah. His final words were of you. He said, 'Tell Sarah I will always love her.'"

Sarah leaned into the strength of Mark's shoulder and sobbed. Mark held her gently and let her cry.

"You're not alone, Sarah. I'm not leaving, especially after seeing a group of Indians pass by on the way back to the house. But right now, we have to build a coffin to put Samuel to rest," Mark said in a whisper.

****

"Indians?" Sarah's mind kept darting from, *what should I do first to what will I do without Samuel?* And then the thought of Indians tied her stomach tighter in knots. Taking a deep breath to slow her racing heart, the words Mark said sank in. She pulled a handkerchief from her apron pocket and dried her tears. Knowing Mark wouldn't be leaving right away gave her some comfort. "Yes," she said. "Build a coffin." The words came out, but she wasn't sure how.

In the last few months, Sarah learned what grief could do to her, and she realized for Jack and Lydia's sake, she didn't want that to happen again. *What to do first?* "Mark, I have to tell Lydia and Jack what happened. The news will be hard for them for they love their father so very much. They must wonder what's keeping me. Lydia already suspects something is wrong."

"Could you fetch some of Samuel's clothes first? Once I've washed and dressed him, you can come out with the children and say your good-byes."

"Yes, washed and dressed." Sarah walked slowly to the house and past Lydia and Jack sitting at the kitchen table and straight to her and Samuel's bedroom.

"Is everything all right?" Sarah heard Lydia call after her.

"We'll talk, Lydia, but Momma has something she must do first." Sarah tried to reassure her daughter. She chose Samuel's favorite shirt and a pair of his trousers, gathered a blanket to wrap around him, and took his good plaid scarf from the hook to wrap around his neck. *No need for the children to see the wound.* She could smell Samuel on the wool. How could she make it through this? Tears threatened to spill, but she brushed them away.

Sarah opened the top drawer of the bureau and found the last handkerchief in the pile was the special one she'd made for Samuel when they were courting. She'd stitched their initials in one corner and Samuel carried it the day they wed. She remembered he dried her tears with it saying good-bye to their families on the day they joined the wagon train. Then, the day the family arrived at the land here in Kansas, he offered it again to dry her tears of joy. Now, remembering those occasions that meant so much to both of them, tears spilled down her cheeks.

She said a quick prayer asking God for strength to see her through the trials ahead. Rolling everything up in a blanket, Sarah headed for the door. Lydia's face held a questioning look and Sarah assured her, "Momma will answer all your questions very soon, but for now you and Jack must both stay in the house. Please."

In the barn, Mark built a simple pine box. Sarah held a board for him as he nailed. "The children won't understand why their father was taken from them. If their momma can't, how can God expect two young children to deal with everything?" She grabbed another board from the pile.

"Tell them their father loved them and he didn't want to leave them this way. Tell them he was a brave man and wanted the best for them. His life ended unexpectedly and he was taken without warning.

"Remind them he is still with them and will watch over them. If they ever want to talk to him they can, like they talk to God in their prayers. He's not here on earth anymore, but he's with them in spirit. As long as they remember him, his memory will live on. That's what my mother told me after my father died."

Sarah stopped crying, absorbing Mark's comforting words.

He continued, "It will be difficult for you and the children, Sarah. After my father was killed in that logging accident, my mother and I struggled for a long time." Mark sighed, "It wasn't easy, but we made it and you and Jack and Lydia will make it too."

"Go be with them, Sarah. I'm almost finished here."

"Let me see him again one more time."

Mark unwrapped the blanket so only Samuel's head was revealed.

Sarah took his face in her hands and gently kissed each closed eye, his nose, and then his lips one last time. *Samuel used to say goodnight with this same kiss when we were courting.*

"We'll bury him by the elm tree. Samuel let the elm stand when we broke ground for the house. He said it would be a shame to cut down a tree that size. It had been there longer than he'd been alive and, as long as he owned the land, it would stay standing. It's the perfect location for Samuel to rest, right beside Baby Walter and my brother Richard."

Sarah's memory returned to the day Samuel made their baby's coffin. Her heart ached remembering the baby boy she lost. Oh, how she wanted that baby and now she lost the baby's father. She let out a long sigh. A calming peace surrounded her and she returned to the house to the difficult task ahead, leaving Mark to wash and dress Samuel and finish the coffin and cross marker.

In the house, the children ran to greet her. Sarah said, "Come sit with me, children. I have to tell you what happened to your father while he and Mark were hunting." By the time she was finished, they were holding each other and crying. Sarah hugged them close to console them, dried their tears with her apron and prayed aloud, "Dear Lord, please take care of Samuel for us until some day we all meet again in Heaven. We know he is with you now and he has no pain. Thank you for the time you allowed him to be in our lives and please know he was a good father and a good husband and we will miss him very much. Amen. We'll lay your father to rest by the old elm on the knoll beside your brother and uncle." Sarah motioned with her hand in the direction of the elm tree.

At that moment, Mark entered the house and nodded to Sarah and the children.

"Let's go say our good-byes." Sarah's voice was barely a whisper. Solemnly they put on their coats and walked hand-in-hand to the barn.

The children were trying to be strong, but when Lydia looked at her poppa lying in the coffin, she ran to him and cried, "Oh, Pa!" Jack cried too, touching his father's face in disbelief.

With a child on each side of their father, Sarah knelt at the foot of the coffin and said a prayer to comfort them, "Dear Lord, be with us as we say good-bye to our Samuel. We are thankful Mark was with Samuel in his final hours, and he was not alone. We regret his family couldn't tell him how much we love him and how much we will miss him now that he is gone from this earth. Give us strength to carry on in our time of sorrow. We know Samuel is with You in Heaven, and he is looking down on us right now and smiling. We know he loved each of us and we know he was proud to be our father, husband, and friend. Amen." After saying their final tearful good-byes, Sarah and the children returned to the house.

Sarah took the family Bible from the shelf and the children gathered as she wrote the entry for Samuel's death: Samuel Thomas Clark, July 21, 1827 – March 24, 1858.

****

Mark said his own final farewell as he carved the cross marker with Samuel's information, vowing once again to keep his promises to his dear friend. He took one long last look at the man he called friend before he nailed the lid on the coffin and walked to the house to ask Jack for help digging the grave.

He and Jack took picks and shovels to the baby's gravesite, dug carefully, and lifted the little coffin out of its shallow bed. Then Mark had an idea. They would dig the grave deep enough to bury both coffins in the same hole.

Few words were spoken as they dug. By mid-afternoon they had dug the baby's grave deep and large enough for both coffins. Carrying the small wooden box to the wagon, Mark and Jack returned to the house. They placed Samuel's coffin alongside the baby's in the back of the wagon and then walked to the house to collect Sarah and Lydia so they could observe the final burial of Samuel and the baby.

Mark looked on with a heavy heart as Sarah and the children walked to the barn. Sarah clutched the family Bible close to chest.

At the wagon, laden with the both coffins, Sarah looked at Mark.

Mark quickly took Sarah aside out of earshot of the children and explained, "Sarah, what if we place the baby in with Samuel instead of burying them side by side? And if you don't like that idea we could bury them in the same grave. Jack and I dug it large enough for both coffins."

Sarah closed her eyes and took a deep breath, letting it out slowly. "Oh, could we? It will give me peace in my heart to know our baby is safe with his father, cradled in his arms for eternity. Samuel would approve, I'm sure. This way, my memories will be of them together, forever."

"We can do whatever you like, Sarah," Mark said, his head hung low.

Sarah ran to the house and returned with a baby quilt. Mark loosened the lids on both coffins while Sarah explained to the children what they were doing. Mark lifted the lid from the baby's coffin first. When he peered inside, there lay a small form swaddled in a blanket. He wrapped the tiny bundle in the quilt Sarah offered and placed the baby in Sarah's arms.

Sarah held her second son close to her heart one last time and kissed the quilt before reluctantly placing him in Samuel's protective arms. Knowing Samuel would always hold Walter close, Sarah was at peace. It all seemed right.

Sarah wore the same black shawl over her coat she'd wore the day they buried Baby Walter. There would be no minister to pray over the bodies. There wasn't for the baby's funeral either, but Samuel and

Walther were with God. She didn't need anyone to reassure her. Anyone who knew Samuel would say he was a good man. He took good care of his family, loved his wife and children, and helped others whenever possible.

Lydia and Jack said, "God be with you," then Sarah took one last look. Seeing Samuel and the baby together she said, "You're both in God's loving hands now." She patted Walter's quilt and gave Samuel one last kiss on the forehead then whispered, "You'll always be my first true love, Samuel."

Mark nailed the lid shut. The family walked beside as Mark drove the wagon to the old elm tree. Using ropes, Mark and Jack carefully lowered the plain box to its final resting place.

"Lydia, would you lead us in song?" Sarah touched her daughter's shoulder.

Lydia sang *Rock of Ages* and *Holy, Holy, Holy! Lord God Almighty*, two of Samuels's favorite hymns. At first, the young girl's voice was barely audible, but once she got to the chorus, she stood tall and her angelic voice rang clear.

"Thank you, Lydia. Your father loved your voice and always loved to hear you sing." Sarah then read from the family Bible,

"The Lord is my shepherd;
I shall not want.
He maketh me to lie down in green pastures:
he leadeth me beside the still waters.
He restores my soul:
he leadeth me in the paths of righteousness for his
name's sake.
Yea, though I walk through the valley of the

shadow of death, I will fear no evil:
   for thou art with me;
   thy rod and thy staff they comfort me.
   Thou preparest a table before me in the presence of
my enemies:
   thou anointest my head with oil;
   my cup runneth over.
   Surely goodness and mercy shall follow me all the
days of my life:
   and I will dwell in the house of the Lord forever."

Sarah picked up a handful of dirt and crumbled it, letting it fall onto the coffin. "We will all miss you, Samuel." Tears could not be held back and streamed down her cheeks. One after the other, each person took a handful of dirt and let it fall, saying a final farewell. After a few moments, Sarah prayed again, "Father in Heaven, we know You welcome Samuel and Baby Walter into Your loving arms and that they are with You in Your heavenly embrace. Give us the strength to carry on and do Your work until You call us home to be with You. We love and will miss Samuel and Walter terribly, but we know they are with You, Lord, and they have eternal life. Hear our prayer, Lord. Amen."

Lydia began to cry and Jack took her hand. Mark began to pound the cross with Samuel's name on it into the ground. The makeshift marker would do until a proper one could be made. Then he caught a glimpse of Jack's face and handed the rock to Jack who finished setting the cross into the earth.

Sarah took Lydia's hand and they walked back to the house to prepare supper while Mark and Jack stayed to close the grave.

****

"Things will change around here now, Jack," Mark said. "You'll have more responsibilities, but your family will be fine," Mark told him.

Mark and Jack brought the wagon back to the barn, stopping in front of the barn doors. "I'll give you children and your mother some time together, Jack." Mark jumped down to open the barn doors.

Jack ran to the house and soon Sarah called out, "Supper's ready."

When Mark walked in the fragrant smells of a comforting hot meal greeted him. His last meal was breakfast yesterday morning.

Sarah made an effort to eat a few bites, and the children, being children, ate heartily as did Mark. After all, food sustained life and they would need their strength for the days ahead. With little conversation during the meal, when Mark's fork touched the plate for the last time, the children jumped up and cleared the table. No arguments occurred over whose turn to wash or dry dishes tonight. Mark tackled the chores and Sarah found herself sitting in her rocking chair holding the family Bible, looking for comfort.

****

Sarah climbed the ladder, tucked the children into bed, and said prayers. A difficult day came to an end and everyone needed rest.

When she kissed Jack goodnight, his strong resemblance to his father overwhelmed her. Sarah gave him a hug to let him know everything would be all right and said, "Sweet dreams." She remembered the way Samuel said those same words...words he would never speak again.

When she comforted Lydia, she could see her

daughter's tear-filled eyes. "I know you miss your poppa, dear. We all miss him and will continue to miss him. We still have each other and all the good memories your poppa gave us. Always remember he loved you and Jack very much."

Lydia sniffled and Sarah tenderly kissed away her tears.

"We'll be fine. It will take time to heal our heartache, but God will be with us every step of the way."

Lydia nodded and snuggled under her blanket.

Sarah kissed her on the cheek, said goodnight, climbed down from the loft, and headed to her rocking chair, tears flowing quietly.

Downstairs, although exhausted, Sarah looked at Mark, and said, "Mark, please, tell me again what happened."

Sarah sat in her rocking chair with a heavy heart as Mark again shared his version of the story, ending with Samuel's final words, the words she longed for Samuel himself to whisper, "Tell Sarah I will always love her."

Hot tears of grief wet her cheeks. She clutched herself tighter to relieve her heartache. She was tired and really needed time alone so she could think. She excused herself for the evening saying, "Mark, you look tired. We can talk more in the morning."

"It's best if I bunk in the barn tonight and tomorrow I'll turn a stall into a place to stow my things. See you in the morning, Sarah."

The awkwardness of the situation couldn't be helped and Sarah was grateful for Mark's thoughtfulness. She always considered him a gentleman.

"As usual, breakfast will be at six," Sarah said, trying to make things seem normal when knowing deep down they could never be that way again.

"Call me when you want me to come in," Mark said. Heading out the door he called, "Goodnight" over his shoulder.

Sarah picked up the lamp and headed to the bedroom. She changed into her nightdress and climbed into the bed she had shared with Samuel. Finally, totally alone for the first time since learning of Samuel's death, she turned her head into the pillow and sobbed uncontrollably.

Chapter Seven

Sarah said good-bye to her husband and baby boy only yesterday. Staying in bed with the covers pulled over her head might be easier than facing the facts, but life must continue. Tears were reserved for private moments now. Life changed once again. Her children depended on her for strength. Her children and the farm were all she had. She didn't know what to do but comfort her children and take it day-by-day.

Frying eggs, she bit her lip. *Oh, how Samuel loved waking to the smell of food cooking.* She pictured him getting dressed, about to come out with a smile on his face and say, "Sure smells good, sweetheart." She wished she could turn back the clock on the last three months and tell Samuel the words she could never tell him again. "I love you, Samuel, we have two wonderful children. Thank you for taking care of us." There were things she hadn't shared with him like blaming herself for their baby's death. Now there could never be another baby. She recalled the nights she didn't let Samuel touch her tenderly to console her and punishing herself for what happened by not returning his affection.

No, forcing herself back to the present. *Now is not the time to indulge in memories. The children need me to be strong to get through the next few months.* She dabbed her apron to her eyes, forcing back tears.

The eggs were ready and the skillet of biscuits where nicely browned when she called the children in the loft and Mark in the barn, "Breakfast is almost on the table. If you want to beat Jack to the food, you'd best hurry."

"Good morning, Mark. Did you sleep all right last night?"

"Not bad, but tonight I'll add more hay to make the bed softer."

"Oh dear. Here, you keep an eye on the eggs while I fetch a quilt. You must have been cold last night."

The children seemed disoriented as they made their way to their chairs. Lydia tied her hair up with a ribbon while Jack pulled his shirt over his head. Out of habit, Sarah set the plates on the table and sat down. While Jack said the prayer, Mark slid the plate from in front of Samuel's chair to in front of himself. Mark had left Samuel's chair empty while he sat in his usual place beside Jack. Sarah's gaze met Mark's and she nodded.

Sarah looked at the children and their tired faces and red eyes looked back. They had cried for the loss of their father last night too. To lighten the mood she said, "Keeping your father's plan of clearing and planting more land this year might be more than the three of us can handle. The work ahead isn't going to be easy, but we can survive if we all work together. We'll need to plant a larger garden this year with Aunt Emma and Uncle Matthew coming. They should be here in time to help with the harvest. It's been four years since we've seen them. They'll be surprised to see how much you both have grown."

"Children, you won't be alone this summer." Mark buttered a biscuit. "My plans are to stay until after the crops are planted and your aunt and uncle arrive. Your father and mother worked hard for this land and your father wanted this family to be self-sufficient. Developing this farm was your father's dream, a dream that can still happen."

A huge burden lifted from Sarah's heart. The Clark family wouldn't lose the farm this year if Mark stayed to help. Thankful for his generosity, tears burned her eyes. Although she hadn't admitted it to herself, she wasn't sure what she and the children would face or could endure without his help until her sister and brother arrived.

"Mark, are you sure you can stay until Emma and Matthew arrive? You would be giving up a cattle drive this spring and work this summer." *Is he really staying? What about Miss Katherine Weaver?*

"Yes, I'll stay, unless you don't want my help."

"No, we want you to stay," Jack blurted out.

"Then it's settled. We'll take a tour around today to figure out what needs to be done and start on the fields tomorrow."

"We'll make Pa's dream come true, won't we Mark?" Jack implored.

Mark nodded to him and then to Lydia glad to see their relieved faces, then looked at Sarah.

****

After breakfast, Mark headed out the door to do the chores. There stood Button, Samuel's horse, at the well. The saddle and reins, covered in mud and grass, hung near the ground.

"Button's home," Mark called out and everyone ran to see.

Mark picked up the reins, took off the bit, and

unfastened the saddle letting them fall. "Thank goodness he found his way home. Come on, Boy, let's get you some food and water." *Thank God my plan worked.* Mark led the weary horse into the barn.

"It's great Button is back, isn't it Mark?" Jack said, running into the barn to check on the horse after chores. "Poppa loved Button. Did those coyotes get him? Is he cut or bleeding?"

"No, he isn't hurt, but he's tired and hungry. He needs a good rub down and his tail is full of burs."

Mark handed Jack the currycomb and left to get a bucket of oats from the storage shed.

When Mark returned, Jack started talking, "I miss Poppa all ready. It's not fair that the Lord took him from us. The other day, after you and Pa left, I almost followed you. I wish I had. I might have saved his life. I've given this a lot of thought and it's my fault. It's my fault Poppa died." The boy's voice trembled as he said these last words, almost making it impossible for him to speak.

"No, Jack. Your father's death was an accident. It's not fair. I agree the Lord took him away too soon. I couldn't stop it from happening. I wish the Lord had taken me instead of your father. I see how much pain you're in. I lost my father when I was about your age. It hurts and it will always hurt, but your father's death was an accident. You mustn't blame yourself."

"I'll have to show Pa I'm the man of the family now. If anybody or anything comes around here to hurt my family, I'll kill them!"

"Jack, please don't ever say that again." Mark's guts wrenched knowing everything Jack believed was based on a lie that he agreed to tell. *Maybe if the family*

*heard Samuel was really a hero for saving the driver
and the orphaned boy's life, they would feel different.*
Mark never imagined Jack's anger would cause such a
rage. He stretched out his arms for Jack to come to him,
but before he could take a step closer, Jack hurled the
horse comb to the floor and ran out. Mark's arms
dropped to his sides. He would give him some time
alone and talk to him again later.

****

Lydia finished her morning chores as Sarah
finished fixing the stew for dinner. "Ma, can you help
me pin the ruffle on my skirt? I need your help to space
it evenly. It has to look perfect, Ma, it just has to. Poppa
picked out this fabric for me. It's the last thing he gave
me, so it has to be perfect even though he'll never see
me wear it."

"He'll see you, sweetheart. Your father loved you
very much. You were his little angel." Sarah knelt on
the floor in front of Lydia and hugged her daughter
close.

Lydia hugged her tight and started crying. "I miss
him, Momma. I miss him so much."

Sarah cupped her daughter's face with her hands
and wiped the tears away. "I know, dear, I miss him
too. And I'm sure Jack and Mark miss him. But don't
worry, Lydia, we'll be all right. Poppa will be with us
in our hearts and any time you want to talk to him, I'm
sure he'll be listening, just like God listens to us. You
heard Mark say he'll stay and help. We'll work
together, one day at a time and we'll survive." Sarah
held her close and then kissed her forehead. "Now, let's
lay out your ruffle and get it pinned."

After pinning every half inch to ease the fabric into

the waistband, Lydia was pleased and threaded a needle to begin stitching.

Sarah forced a smiled as she tied on her bonnet. "Come out to the barn if you need me." She slipped on her coat and walked out the door.

Sarah found Mark brushing Button. "Wasn't Jack here with you?"

"He was, but he took off. He blames himself for his father's death. He feels Samuel should have let him go on the hunting trip. He said his pa would be alive today if he had been there to save him. Now he thinks he has to be the man of the family."

"Death at any age is difficult to deal with, Mark. We don't know what God's plans for us are until they happen. Of course Jack's angry. Maybe Samuel was in error not to let him go along. I can't help thinking if Samuel had stayed home working, or even stayed another day before heading out, maybe this horrible accident wouldn't have happened. But I believe everything happens for a reason. We don't always understand it at the time, but the Lord knows his plan and we cannot judge him or question his decisions." When Sarah looked up, Mark stared at the floor. His face frozen with a somber expression.

"Oh, Mark, my sleeplessness and my own grief have caught up to me. I haven't considered your feelings. You loved Samuel, too. And I know he was looking forward to the hunting trip with you. There was no way he'd ever have let me talk him out of it. We agreed we could use the meat and he always enjoyed your time together. Samuel looked forward to your visits every year."

"I don't blame you for what happened. Samuel's

death was an accident and you did all you could to save him." Now she looked down at the floor. "You're giving up a lot to stay with our family to see us through these hard times. For that I'm very grateful. Once my siblings arrive, you can leave. We couldn't stay in Kansas if they weren't coming."

Mark looked her in the eyes and said, "Then we better get started. Samuel explained his plans to me for this year's crops. He said he never wanted to go through a winter like last year's again." Mark leaned against the spring wagon. "Samuel's dream was to have a self-sufficient farm a few years down the road, but you own enough land to graze a herd of cattle." He took off his hat and ran his fingers through his hair. "He was well on his way before last winter's set-back. He told me about the Indians showing up and wanting meat. Last year took a toll on him. He worried if this year's crops failed, you might lose your farm. I can't let that happen. No, it won't happen."

Chapter Eight

One afternoon, while Lydia sewed, Sarah set out to pack away some of Samuel's clothing in a spare trunk. The same trunk she stored the quilt the church ladies and her mother gave them before they headed west. Each of the woman had stitched their names on the patch they made for the quilt. Her mother had embroidered the word Mother on hers in blue thread. She ran her finger over the letters, hugged the quilt to her chest, and then continued with the task at hand.

Seeing Samuel's clothes hanging in the wardrobe was a daily reminder of her loss. *Besides, perhaps one day Jack could wear them. They're perfectly good clothes. Mark could use them, but they wouldn't fit. Mark's taller and broader in the shoulders than Samuel.*

She lovingly folded every garment and laid it flat in the trunk. The clothes brought back so many memories...good memories. Next, she started on the top drawer of the bureau they shared. She took out one of Samuel's wrinkled nightshirts and buried her face in it. His essence surrounded her and brought her comfort. Smoothing it, she sat with it in her arms on the bed and soon fell into a recollection of old times, even before Jack was born. Sarah wasn't sure how long she'd been musing when she heard Lydia singing a song. The rest could wait. She had done enough for now and placed the nightshirt under Samuel's pillow. After she closed the drawer, she slid the trunk into the corner, and went about the rest of her day.

Samuel's death and burial were less than a week ago. Easter Sunday was the next day. Sarah prepared noodles and bread for the observance, and then walked out to draw water from the well. While waiting for the bucket to fill, she glanced out toward the fields and was startled to see six Indians riding past. They didn't stop or seem to want anything. She froze, petrified and alone at the well.

Samuel always kept a loaded gun in the house, but she never fired it. Now she wished she had learned, although, she questioned if she ever had to pull the trigger whether or not she could. Seeing the Indians so close made Sarah uneasy the rest of the day, especially after the run-in Samuel had with them last winter trying to steal a cow.

That night, after the children were asleep, Sarah told Mark about seeing the Indians. "It isn't safe being alone at the house with Indians so close. It would set my mind at ease if you took Lydia and me with you until the fields are cleared."

"Of course, Sarah. We can use your help if you don't mind picking stones. Stones always need picked and makes the plowing easier every year. Rest assured the Indians who tried to take the cow this past winter were most likely just low on food.

****

On Easter morning after breakfast, Mark and Jack dodged much-needed raindrops running to the barn to do chores. Lydia and Sarah were in the kitchen making pumpkin pies and molasses rich honeycomb pudding.

Once a roast, potatoes, and squash were placed in the oven for a late mid-day meal, the children played a game of checkers at the kitchen table and Sarah busied herself with some sewing.

"I'm going out to take a nap. Call me when it's time to eat." Mark reached for his coat. He wanted to give the Clark family some time alone. The rain stopped and the barn was quiet. His head hitting the pillow was the last he remembered until he heard Sarah calling him for the Easter meal. Afterward, Sarah and Lydia dished up bowls of pumpkin pie with a spoonful of honeycomb molasses pudding on the side for dessert.

Enjoying the special treat, Lydia asked Mark, "Tell us what your family did on Easter when you were young."

As Mark talked, warm memories he hadn't thought of in years flooded his mind. He shared a couple of stories about living in the little town of Tidioute, in Pennsylvania. "Well, there was this one Easter Sunday when the crocuses bloomed on the banks of the Allegheny River early enough to pick. 'They'll make a nice bouquet,' my mother said, and pinned a blossom on her spring coat to wear to church. We always went to church on Easter. I hated having to get cleaned up and wear my good clothes because they didn't fit right." Mark wrinkled his face, twitched his nose and mouth, and then wiggled his body up and down.

Lydia giggled.

"I'll never forget the Sunday my mother surprised me with a necktie. I was probably seven or eight at the time. My father always wore one, but I never figured I'd have one too. My father showed me how to tie it. Then Mother made me wear it every Sunday." Mark chuckled. "I bet she still has it somewhere."

****

After the children finished their dessert, Sarah asked Lydia to fetch her the Bible from the top shelf in the living room. Sarah read aloud the Easter story, from the book of Matthew. When she finished, she encouraged everyone to head to bed early, knowing they would start again tomorrow on the hard work of clearing more land.

The following morning, Sarah announced, "Lydia, you'll wear the oldest pair of trousers your brother owns and one of your old shirts. You and me are going with Mark and Jack to help clear the fields today. Jack, run and fetch your trousers for your sister."

"But, Ma, what good can we do?" Lydia crossed her arms and stood feet apart.

"We'll help with whatever we can. We need to get that land cleared and ready for planting. Now run and get an old shirt."

Lydia stomped off and when she returned, Sarah helped her cinch up the trousers around her waist with a piece of old clothes line and roll the pants legs to length. Day after day in the fields, Sarah and Lydia helped drag brush, pick rocks, and carry manageable branches to the wagon. Time spent clearing the land meant little time for other chores like gathering wood. So, not only did they clear the land, but they also brought firewood home with them every night. Mark cut and stacked it while Sarah made supper and Jack and Lydia tended to the other evening chores.

During the morning wagon rides to the fields, Sarah invented spelling bee games for the children and on the way home, Jack and Lydia practiced their times tables or took turns reading. Mark would get involved sometimes, taking a turn with a spelling word or an arithmetic problem. At least some learning took place during the week. Usually Sarah was strict about studying, but she allowed this type of schooling for now because the work needed to be done.

"Your father would be very proud seeing you both working together to clear our land," she said. "His dream for our farm included increasing our planting so we could be self-sufficient...grow and prosper. He loved getting his hands in the soil this time of year. But now he's watching over us and knows we're doing everything we can to fulfill that dream.

****

On Thanksgiving Day morning, April 13th, bright sunshine from the window on the east end of the house lit the sitting room. After breakfast and morning chores, Mark hitched up the wagon and surprised everyone when he asked, "Who wants to take a break and go for a ride? The wagon is waiting outside."

Sarah and Lydia had already stuffed the turkey Mark shot and all the food for the day's feast were in the oven. "A short ride would be nice." Sarah agreed. The children hurried to grab their coats and everyone jumped into the wagon. After traveling a ways up stream, typically not the direction they journeyed, Mark stopped the wagon and helped Sarah off.

Looking out across the rolling plains as the sun shone through openings in the clouds, Sarah pointed to the distance. "Our land spreads beyond that patch of switch grass way over there. We truly are blessed. With Richard's ground that adjoins ours and the quarter plot of the Henderson's land Samuel bought, we have nine-hundred and sixty acres in all."

"I didn't realize Samuel owned that much land." Mark shaded his eyes and squinted in the direction Sarah pointed.

They spread a blanket and Mark sat on one corner. "We've worked hard up to this point, but it's not over yet. It won't be easy getting the crops in, but Jack is determined. And now with you and Lydia helping, we'll work as a team. Sarah, Samuel would be very proud of his family."

Sarah agreed. "As long as the weather cooperates, we should be in good shape especially since my brother and sister are coming. They should be leaving the middle of May and be here in time to help with the harvest in late August. Their journey will be starting soon. I worry about them traveling alone, but I'm sure they'll be placed with a good family to care for them. They'll be such a help and it will be so good to see them again. The children are looking forward to their arrival."

On the ride home, Sarah began a discussion about Thanksgiving and gave a short history lesson. "A day of thanks and reflection," she said, and then listed things she was thankful for. She kept her list positive saying, "I'm thankful for the people in my life and how much love we all share. I'm thankful for Mark staying with us and for everyone's hard work preparing the fields and garden. Now, if Mother Nature helps out, we're sure to make this a better year."

"Why don't we each take turns to share what we're thankful for? Lydia, will you go next?"

Lydia took a moment and began, "I'm thankful for the nice weather and hope the crops do well so there's enough food for all the cattle next winter. It broke Poppa's heart and mine too when the cow died. Please, God, be with us and watch over us." Then she nodded to Jack to go next.

"I'm grateful for Mark's help with the fields and with Aunt Emma and Uncle Matthew coming, they can help with the harvest. Oh, and I look forward to fishing with Mark after the fields are planted and maybe Mark will teach me how to hunt. I'd be real thankful for that," Jack added as they bumped along the trail back to the house.

Mark spoke last. "I'm grateful as well for everyone's hard work getting the fields cleared. We'll get it done if everyone works as a team. Don't worry, Lydia, we'll plant more crops so the cows will have plenty of feed this winter. I'm praying for bountiful crops, rain to sustain them, and a light winter ahead. And don't worry, Jack. I'm sure there will be plenty of time for fishing and hunting." Mark smiled and gave Sarah a wink.

****

After feasting on turkey with all the trimmings, Sarah suggested, "Let's walk up to the graves for some evening air before we eat dessert." Although still difficult to make that walk, Sarah forced herself. *It's necessary for the children so they don't forget their father is always with them.*

Lydia skipped ahead and picked some spring flowers to place at the foot of each grave. Jack quickly straightened his poppa's cross after seeing the ground settled and the cross tipped.

Mark walked to the edge of the meadow and picked up a rock. "Let's see if we can find some rocks to help prop up the cross so it stands straighter."

While Mark and the children looked for rocks, Sarah spent a few minutes with Samuel. Standing by his grave always made Sarah feel a closer connection with him even though she knew in her heart he was no longer present. Silently she told Samuel that Mark staying on was a blessing, her siblings would arrive by harvest, and then Mark could return to Miss Katherine and get on with his life.

Jack pounded the stones they found into the ground around the cross.

"Good work." Sarah assured him.

"I miss you, Pa." Lydia knelt at the cross.

"Me too." Jack nodded.

Sarah recited the Lord's Prayer and the children and Mark joined in.

****

Sarah and the children helped with the plowing in the cool of the mornings. Afternoons, Mark and Jack worked on enlarging the corral and building troughs. After days of coming home tired and hungry with sunburns and calloused hands, the wood house bulged at the seams and noticeable progress was seen in the fields.

Some evenings they would return to the fields after supper. Working together, they completed the projects Samuel never finished before that fateful hunting trip in March. As much as Sarah now wished she'd told Samuel not to go hunting that day, she couldn't have denied him the time with his friend and the pleasure of hunting. His death was an accident. She accepted that fact, but her heart still ached. She longed for his touch, a whisper of his voice one last time, and found herself looking for him to walk through the door or to lie beside her at night.

Chapter Nine

Mark needed Sarah to continue to place her trust in him. Would the lies stop at two? First Samuel's death and now collecting the reward.

The bank must be sitting on the reward money. It's been over five weeks. I can't wait any longer, or the sheriff might begin to wonder. The details were vivid after memorizing Samuel's last conversation. Convincing the sheriff that he was Samuel was all that stood in the way.

He took Sarah aside in the kitchen after supper and explained, "Sarah, there's something I must take care of and it will take me away for four or five days. Are there any supplies you need from town? If so, make a list and I'll pick them up on my way through. I hope you know I wouldn't leave unless I had too. It's important." He took her hand in his. "Will you and the children be all right?

"Yes, we'll be fine, Mark. You go." Her knees weakened and Sarah leaned against the counter as dizziness overcame her. She slipped her hand from Mark's and gently placed it on his shoulder. "We'll be fine," she said again, "but you will come back, won't you, Mark?" She gazed into his eyes awaiting his answer.

"Yes. I'll be back as soon as I can." Leaving Sarah alone could cause her a setback, but without the reward money, Samuel's death would be for naught.

Sarah started to tear. "I promise I'll return, Sarah. I promise." He hated to leave. She appeared so vulnerable, but the reward money wouldn't wait forever.

Mark remembered Samuel telling him about Sarah's state of mind after losing the baby. She didn't seem to be falling into that dark place, but Mark needed to be reassured. Still looking her directly in the eyes, he asked once again. "Are you sure you'll be all right for a few days, you and the children?"

Sarah nodded.

Later that evening, while cutting wood, Mark talked to Jack, "It's up to you to help your mother while I'm gone. If anything happens your mother cannot handle, or if there's trouble, ride to the neighbors for help."

Jack nodded in understanding.

Mark didn't question they'd be fine, but made sure Jack understood his responsibilities giving him the opportunity to be the man of the house.

****

Sarah sat at the table, paper, pen and ink well in front of her, prepared once again to share sad news with her mother. She longed for the strength of Samuel's reassurance. *What if Mark doesn't come back? The crops aren't in yet. Mark promised he'd help us. He must intend to return.*

In the back of her mind she suspected Mark's trip was to see Miss Katherine Weaver. She couldn't blame him but wanted him to come back to the farm. Samuel had told her about Katherine, but she was curious now why Mark hadn't said anything.

A tear dropped onto her paper. Blotting it dry with her sleeve, Sarah dipped the pen in ink and began her letter to her mother.

April 18, 1858
Northwest Border, Riley County Kansas
Dearest Mother,

Sarah's mind raced as she tried to find the words to express her loss. Four months since the loss of Baby Walter and as she still questioned, *why would the Lord do this to me? He took my baby and then my husband.* She struggled with fatigue and waves of grief, but she held together for the children's sake.

There have been several things happening here, one right after the other and I am afraid I have terrible news to share yet again. By this time you received word about the loss of our baby boy on January 10th. It is with a heavy heart that I now must tell you I have also lost Samuel to an unfortunate accident that occurred while he was hunting with a friend on March 24. Samuel tripped and fell on an outcrop of rocks. When he fell, a sharp rock punctured his neck and Mark Hewitt, who was with him, could not stop the bleeding. Mark loved him like a brother and I trust he did everything he could for Samuel.

I feel so alone without Samuel. I still feel his presence and see him walking through the door when I call the family to a meal. My heart aches for one more kiss. I never got to tell him 'I love you', one last time. I miss his smile and the way he made me feel when he would say, 'Everything will be all right.'

Sarah trembled uncontrollably. She put the pen down. Writing about her profound loss she relived the feeling afresh. *We had so many plans, so much we* wanted to share and accomplish. Now he won't get to see Jack and Lydia grow up or meet his grandchildren. Letting out a sigh she picked up the pen again.

The children miss him too, and of course they don't understand why God took him away. It breaks my heart to see their sad faces when they realize the things they did with their father, they will never get a chance to do with him again.

We are all trying to be strong and carry on without him, but it is grievously difficult. Mark helped us bury Samuel. He dug the baby's grave large enough for Samuel's coffin too. Then we did something that just seemed right. We opened Samuel's coffin and laid the baby in his arms and buried the two of them together. I am sure Samuel approves. It warms my heart to think they are together forever.

What about Samuel's mother? *Polly will take this hard, of course. This is not the kind of news to learn about in a letter. Besides, she needs someone with her when she hears. Samuel was her only son. My mother should tell her.*

Polly will be devastated when she is told the news. It would be better if she learned about her son from a person who knew and loved him as I know you did. I hope Polly is comforted to know that Mark was the one who was with him when the accident occurred. Mark said he tried everything he could, but he could not save Samuel.

The children are upset, of course, and Jack is feeling guilty for not being there to take care of his father on the hunting trip. Both Mark and I assured Jack even if he were there the outcome would be the same.

I have given it great thought. My light of hope is that Emma and Matthew will be here soon. With Emma and Matthew's help we will be able to keep the farm and stay in Kansas. With all of our heartache and sadness right now, it is a blessing they will be coming this summer.

Thank God for Mark. I am not sure what we would have done without his willingness to stay and see us through the planting season. But I am sure he will be anxious to leave once the children arrive.

Please pray for us, Mother. Pray God will heal our broken hearts and give us strength to carry on without Samuel in our lives. Pray for a good growing season and harvest so we can keep the farm.

It's hard to be strong for my children's sake. *If only you were here with us, Mother.* If only.

So many times I wished we lived closer. I miss you and all the talks we shared, all the advice you gave me, and all the love that pours from your heart. Please tell Father and the children how much we miss them too and give them kisses from me.

I must close now. Thank you for telling Polly for me, Mother. Please tell her the children and I love her very much. I will write again soon.

Your loving daughter,
Sarah

That evening, handing Mark the addressed envelope, Sarah asked, "Would you mail this letter for me when you're in town?"

"Of course, Sarah." Mark slipped it in his pocket.

"Fever medicine is really the only thing we need from town. I appreciate your willingness to pick it up. When the whole family goes to town, Samuel always asked Seth Frazer to care for the livestock. Have you ever met Seth?"

"No, the name doesn't sound familiar. Where is his place?"

"As the crow flies, it's only about ten or twelve miles northwest of here. He has a house with a quarter plot of ground. His wife died on the wagon train trip west and he was heartbroken. With no children, he never remarried. He does for himself and comes to visit us occasionally, maybe once or twice a year. Other than that, we think he pans for gold over near the Smokey Hill River."

"Samuel usually rode over to Seth's and back the same day. He'd visit a few hours to catch Seth up on the news from town. Seth's another person who doesn't want anything to do with politics and disapproves of slavery as we do. He doesn't go to town much. We pick up essentials for him when we go and he pays us when he can."

"Someday maybe we'll get a chance to meet."

"I'm sure you will if you stay around long enough." Sarah smiled. "Here's money to mail the letter and pay for the medicine. And, as a surprise for the children would you please ask the clerk to make up two, one-cent bags of candy? Maybe it will help cheer them a little." A silver half dollar was all she dare spend from her money jar, money she saved from selling eggs and vegetables on the rare occasions she got to town. "You'll have to charge the rest, Mark. We don't have the money right now, but our credit should be good. Put the rest on our bill."

Sarah didn't have a clue that credit might not be an option. They said goodnight and Mark walked to the barn.

Chapter Ten

After a few hours of sleep, Mark hitched Ruby to the spring wagon and by the light of the moon headed out. He needed to get to Dead Flats before the bank closed plus, he wanted to see if Samuel's bedroll with his bloodied clothes were still buried where he'd left them by the creek. Two miles from the ranch, Mark approached the creek and the moonlit grove of trees. Would the bedroll still be buried under the brush? As he approached, his heart began to race. The brush hadn't been disturbed. He took it as a good sign.

His skin crawled at the notion of someone finding the evidence. Traces of that day must never be found. He tied Ruby to some brush, grabbed the shovel from the back of the wagon, and quickly set to work digging.

As he tamped down the earth on the newly dug deeper hole and covered the area with brush, a slight headache at his temples and a feeling of guilt swept over him, the same guilt overwhelmed him when he lied to Sarah about Samuel's death. One lie would now be compounded by another…the reward money.

Sarah worried about every penny she spent. If he was successful collecting the reward money, his plan was to buy additional supplies and then pay all store debts. He'd also pick up some lumber and buy barley and rye grass in addition to the seed Samuel had already purchased.

****

Mark arrived at Dead Flats just before the bank closed. He wouldn't normally ride Ruby so hard, but he needed to open a bank account before he left for Marysville early the next morning.

In the bank, Mark walked to the teller, took out his money pouch, and counted out twenty dollars. "I'd like to open an account," he stated. Mark slid the money under the cage in front of the bank worker and signed the necessary papers. Returning the pen to its holder, Mark asked, "If I had money wired to my account here, how much time would it take if the bank was in Kansas?"

The teller cleared his throat. "The person wiring the money would need your account number and then it takes only one day to process the transfer. So, if money was sent to this bank before one in the afternoon, the following day it would be available for withdrawal."

"Thank you. You've been most helpful." Mark wrote his account number on a piece of paper and tucked it in his shirt pocket.

The next stop was the postal office. Mark pulled two letters from his pocket. Sarah's letter to her mother and his letter to Miss Katherine letting her know he was fine, not to worry, and to tell her about his friend's death. *So much has happened. I wonder, does she miss me?* But everything had changed and his life had to be put on hold, at least for the immediate future.

The next morning, leaving the wagon and Ruby at the stable, he paid for a horse to ride northeast to Marysville. Ruby needed a break so when he returned he could travel speedily back to Sarah and the children.

He wanted this second lie behind him and only a

face-to-face with the sheriff could make that happen.

Once in Marysville, Mark found the sheriff's office, dismounted and tethered the horse. Before going in, he wiped the sweat from his face with his sleeve and took a deep breath. He had his part of the story impressed in his mind.

Mark opened the door. The smell of stale tobacco smoke hit him in the face. Glancing around the room, two cells lined the back wall along with a rifle cabinet, locked with a steel bar across it. Behind the desk sat the sheriff in a slouched position, head down with his arms folded over his paperwork. Beside the desk was a spittoon.

The door creaked when it closed; the sheriff raised his head and rubbed his eyes. "Can I help you?" he said in a gruff voice probably from too many shots of rotgut whiskey.

Mark took off his hat and ran his fingers through his hair. "Sheriff, my name's Mark Hewitt. I've come to collect the reward for the two men who tried to hold up the stage a few weeks back. They did have a bounty on their heads, didn't they, Sheriff?"

The sheriff nodded, "Yup. Come to find out they were a gang wanted for a couple of robberies."

The sheriff stroked his salt-and-pepper chin stubble and rubbed his eyes again. It was obvious he was just waking up, even though the time was already mid-day.

"Sorry I couldn't get here sooner," Mark said, "but I had things to tend to that couldn't wait."

The sheriff looked Mark up and down and walked around the desk to shake his hand.

"Reed Kurtz, Sheriff of Marysville. Call me Reed." Mark shook Reed's hand.

"Glad you got here when you did, Mark. Good timing. The money was wired just yesterday. Come far?"

"Rode in from Dead Flats today. Did the driver tell you about the robbery? After I stopped to help, all hell broke loose."

"Why, yes, good ole Buck told me everything. Said he thought you were a farmer and your calloused hand tells me he was right."

"What happened to the boy in the stage?" Mark hesitated. "I think his father called him Willy?"

A voice in his head suddenly whispered, *Billy*.

"No, sorry." Mark shook his head. "The boy's name is Billy. Yes, Billy's what his father called him. He has a birthmark on his neck. How's the young lad doing? Sorry he lost his Pa and all. Hope you were able to get him back home to his family."

"Well, it wasn't that easy." the sheriff scratched his face. "Billy Henry and his father used to live in Kansas City. His mother was dead and he didn't have any relatives, so we found someone to take him. He's fine."

"What about the driver? Is his arm on the mend?"

"Ole Buck is doing fine. He told me to thank you for him, although he should be rolling in here soon and can do it himself. He sure was glad you showed up that day and so was the bank. They sent along a little extra something to express their appreciation." Reed smiled. "Gosh, I can't remember if Buck said where you were heading that day and what you were doing when you happened upon the broken down stage." The sheriff returned to his chair and crossed his feet on the corner of the desk, ready to pass judgement on this stranger.

Mark anticipating these questions pulled up a chair.

"Well, an old friend and I were heading to Blue Rapids hoping to get a couple deer before planting season. Last year's hard winter set us back a little." Mark glanced at the old clock on the wall. It read eleven-thirty. Was the time right? Five minutes off either way and it could cost him everything. His heart began to beat faster and sweat threatened to belie his supposed ease. *If Buck's coming, things better hurry along here. How many more questions will it take for him to believe me?*

The sheriff picked up on his glance at the clock and asked, "Are you staying in town?"

"No, got to get back home, left my little woman alone with the children. She frets when I'm away. Got a long ride ahead of me."

Mark had to get out of the sheriff's office and Marysville before Buck arrived. To speed things up, he decided to tell the sheriff everything else he knew. He blurted out, "A good thing the spokes on that wheel didn't break when it came off. With the three of us lifting and the boy there to slide it back in position, we got the job done. It sure was a hot one that day."

Seemingly satisfied with Mark's recounting, the sheriff said, "C'mon, we'll walk over to the bank so you can get your money straight away." As they walked the wooden walkway toward the bank, Reed said, "There's only one more question I need to ask."

But I don't have any more answers. Mark's expression went blank waiting for the question.

Reed turned and looked him in the eyes. "Where was your friend when you stopped and helped?"

Mark's answer brought back the painful truth with a rush of guilt. "My friend forgot his canteen when we stopped for a break earlier, about three miles back. He returned to retrieve it and I hunted my way along the path. That's when I ran upon the stage and offered to help. Everything was all right when I left. I worried my friend heard the shots and might've thought I was in trouble."

"Well, that makes sense." Reed scratched his head.

Opening the door to the Marysville Bank, Mark followed the sheriff, trying to give off an air of confidence. All he could think was, *"This is it. This is the big moment."* He wiped the sweat that suddenly appeared on his forehead with his shirtsleeve while the sheriff's back was turned.

"Victor in today?" The sheriff asked one of the tellers who nodded and pointed to the hallway.

The sheriff knocked on the door with "President" written on it and entered without waiting for an invitation.

"This is Victor Barns, Bank President," the sheriff said to Mark, "And Victor, this here is Mark Hewitt, the man you're holding the reward money for."

The next few minutes would decide everything.

Victor, a tall gentleman in his early fifties, stood to shake Mark's hand across his desk.

"So, you're the man who saved Buck's life." Victor looked at Mark. "He sure sang your praises. Said he didn't know what he'd done if you hadn't coming along when you did."

"I'm just sorry the boy's father was killed," Mark said, not knowing what else to say.

"Well, Sheriff, if this is the right man, the paperwork's right here and ready to be signed. We could wait for Buck if you have any doubts. We'd hate to make a mistake and give this much money to the wrong person." Victor smiled.

"No, we have the right guy." The sheriff slapped Mark on the back. "Besides, who would be as bold as to ride in here and pretend to be someone they weren't. He's told me things only the witness of the robbery could know."

Mark held his breath thinking, the only thing Buck hadn't mentioned was the scar on my left cheek. He prayed it wouldn't give him away.

"If you say so, Sheriff." Victor extended a pen, uncapped the ink well, and slid it forward for Mark to use.

Mark stepped to the desk, palms damp. He dipped the pen in the ornate inkwell, careful not to spill a drop. His eyes grew wide when he read the amount on the document was twelve hundred dollars, more money than he imagined.

Mark paused. This was his last chance to change his mind. He took a breath to calm himself. There would be no going back if he signed this paper. The words were a blur. He really should read the document, but instead he took a deep breath and somehow he steadied his hand. With his best handwriting, he signed, Mark C. Hewitt.

"Could you wire this to the bank in Dead Flats for me," he said, with a confidence in his voice that surprised even himself and returned the pen to its rest.

Mark wanted to leave. How much longer must he stay? He took another deep breath and tried to stay calm. Would he hear the stage approach from inside the bank? If Buck got a look at him, everything was over. Instead of heading back to the farm, he'd be heading to jail and explaining the truth to Sarah in a letter. The same truth that, according to Samuel, would break her heart.

"Do you know your account number?" Victor asked.

"Yes, I have it right here." Mark handed Victor the paper he had tucked in his shirt pocket yesterday at the Dead Flat's bank.

"You're smart not carrying this much cash." Victor leaned back in his chair.

"This money will change our lives." Mark unconsciously scratched his cheek, then realized *Oh no, my scar*. He hurriedly said, "Now my family can rest easier if this year's crops don't fare so well."

"Thanks for everything, Gentlemen." Mark looked at Victor. "Can you send it right away, so the money will be at the bank in Dead Flats tomorrow morning? I need to pick up some supplies."

"Yes, it'll be there," Victor replied. "I'll wire it right now."

"Great." Mark glanced at the regulator clock on the wall. *Oh, no, ten minutes to twelve. Time to get moving.* He shook hands with the two men, and said, "Thanks for everything." When Mark and the sheriff exited the bank, he wanted to jump on his horse and take off, get as far away from Marysville as possible, and never look back. But instead, he shook the sheriff's hand again, and said, "Thanks, Reed. Tell Buck 'Sorry' for me. Maybe we'll meet up again. Under different circumstances, of course." Mark forced a smile.

With that, Mark ran his fingers through his hair, put on his hat, and tried to walk calmly back to where his livery horse stood waiting. He mounted and looked to see if the sheriff watched which way he left town.

The sheriff had already walked back to his office. Mark quickly rode down the closest alley to avoid any chance of being seen by Buck when he barreled into town.

Buck's running late, but my leaving town before he arrives is unwise. My scar could give me away. What if the sheriff questions Buck about it? Funny, a lie got me that scar in the first place and now another lie could send me to prison.

Mark sat on his horse alongside a brick building at the edge of town with a clear view of Main Street. *Samuel looked out for me. All the details Samuel told me were important, but when he whispered the boy name to me, knowing the boy's name was Billy made all the difference to the sheriff. That sure was a close call.*

A few tense minutes later, the stagecoach arrived and after it passed, Mark rode out. Once out of town, he picked up the pace and looked back every so often to make sure the sheriff wasn't behind him.

He let out a long sigh of relief. *But what if the sheriff shows up at the bank in Dead Flats tomorrow? They might discover by then they made a mistake. Can't quite say I've pulled it off until the money is in my pocket. It'll be a long restless night.*

****

Mark camped the night a few miles outside of Dead Flats and rode in early the next morning. He returned the horse to the stables, hitched Ruby to the wagon, paid the livery bill, and walked to the Wild Rose Hotel for breakfast. He ate heartily, figuring it could be his last meal as a free man.

Waiting at the bank for it to open, Mark wondered, *would the Dead Flat's sheriff be waiting inside?* The door was unlocked and he approached the teller's window. The teller was a different person from yesterday. Sweat broke out on Mark's brow.

"Hello, my name is Mark Hewitt and here is my account number." He slid the paper through the cage. "Can you tell me my account balance, please?"

The teller checked his ledger, wrote the amount on a piece of paper, and slid it to Mark. All twelve hundred dollars plus the twenty dollars he used to open the account was there. No questions were asked and Mark made a withdrawal. Letting out a long anticipated sigh of relief as he walked out the door, he'd done it. He managed to pass as Samuel and collect the reward.

Money in hand, he headed to the dry goods store first where he purchased fancy blue fabric for Sarah, and a pink flowered print fabric for Lydia, asking the clerk for enough of each to make two dresses. He also requested matching lace for both and fever medicine.

"Would you like a copy of the newest *Godey Ladies* magazine?" The clerk smiled. "We have a back issue I can sell you." She smiled again, trying to make another sale.

"Yes, please add it to my pile." Mark motioned to the counter and then searched for a surprise for Jack. A leather coin pouch was his final decision and he placed a shiny Liberty silver dollar inside.

Mark strolled past the shelves along the wall and picked up a tin of cocoa, a small jug of maple syrup, a tin of molasses, and twenty pounds each of coffee beans, cornmeal, flour, and sugar. The last things he added to his stack of provisions were four books the children would enjoy. He'd save them as a surprise for a rainy day.

"Would you please make up two, two-cent candy

bags and be sure to include some rock candy, stick candy and lemon drops." A tall slender man adding up his bill nodded. "I'll be back shortly to pay for everything. I have to head over to the hardware store for a minute."

There, Mark asked the storekeeper, "Got any barley and rye seed left? Need enough to plant an acre of each, and a keg of ten-penny nails and some pine lumber. I need about one hundred board feet if you have any."

"Yup, got the seed and nails right here. The lumber's out back. There isn't much. Load up what you want and I'll give you a good price on it," replied the clerk, an older gentleman.

Mark secured the goods in the wagon, returned to pay, and was almost out the door when the old man asked, "Are you new to this area?"

Mark, aware that this might happen, froze in the doorway and answered, "No, I'm not. This is for Sarah Clark," he explained. "Sorry to say her family had great losses this year. Samuel and I were on a hunting trip when we had a run in with some coyotes after Samuel shot a deer. Then the horse must have smelled them and galloped away. Samuel even joked, 'Ole Button never did like coyotes. Darn, now I'll have to go chase him down.'"

"Yep, that sounds like Samuel," the old man said.

"Then Samuel tripped and fell backward hitting hard on an outcropping of rocks. One punctured his neck. There was no stopping the bleeding and before long he was gone."

"Gosh, that's awful. Samuel was a good man." The clerk wrung his hands.

"Yes, and a mighty good friend," Mark added, shifting his stance slightly. He was sure the news of Samuel's fate would circulate around town quickly. He swore from that day forward he'd never lie except to keep the secret of Samuel's death and what he would tell Sarah about the newly acquired money.

"I think I've seen you before, young fella. You and Samuel were here in town last month, weren't you?"

"That's right. Rode in from Missouri to meet him. We grew up together back in Pennsylvania. I'm staying with Miz Clark long enough to help get her fields planted. Can't have Sarah lose her farm. Her two children and the farm are all she has now. She's hoping for good crops this year and a light winter."

The clerk nodded his head in agreement. "Please convey my sympathy to Miz Clark."

Back at the dry goods store, Mark told the owner, "I'll pay for today's bill and I'd like to pay off Samuel Clark's debt as well. Please check your records and tell me the amount."

After going through his account ledger, the owner said, "That'll be thirty-one dollars, Sir."

Mark counted out the money and asked for a receipt. The owner wrote "Paid in Full" in the store ledger and on the receipt which he handed to Mark. A weight suddenly lifted from Mark's shoulders. One of Samuel's debts was paid. He'd pay off the hardware debt next trip to town. He didn't want it to appear like he was taking Samuel's place or that he had lots of money. Sarah was bound to ask questions. The number of lies he had to remember weighed on Mark. He couldn't make a mistake and still keep his promise to Samuel. Another lie he must tell Sarah and again it must sound believable.

He tied down the sacks in the back of the wagon, making sure all was secure and covered everything with the wool blanket he bought to replace his bedroll buried along with Samuel's bloody clothes.

As Mark drove out of town, he said to Ruby, "Come on girl. Let's get back to the farm."

Mark drove into the farm at dusk the next day. The family had already eaten supper and the evening chores were done. He quickly hid the few surprises he purchased before Jack rushed out to help him unhitch the wagon.

"Ma's been worried about you, Uncle Mark. She saved you some supper. Go eat and I'll finish up out here." Jack started unhitching Ruby from the wagon

Mark, sensing urgency in Jack's voice, asked, "Is everything all right?"

"Everything is fine. Not one problem," Jack insisted.

"I'll eat after I rub down Ruby and feed and water her. She's had a long trip and needs some extra care. You can give me a hand, if you like."

"No, I can do this. You go eat." Jack bumped Mark aside and picked up the water pail.

"Okay, thanks Jack." Mark scooped up as many provisions as he could carry and headed to the house. Just as he stepped onto the porch, Sarah opened the door for him.

Chapter Eleven

"Mark! You're back!" Sarah let out a sigh of relief. "Did everything go all right?" she asked, taking one of the sacks and setting it on the counter.

"No problems. I took it slow on Ruby. We drove straight through with only a few breaks and a couple hours of sleep." Mark set the sacks on the table.

"You must be hungry. Let me dish you up some food."

"There's a couple more sacks to carry in, but yes, some food would taste good."

Sarah filled a bowl with warmed up soup and buttered two slices of bread.

Mark returned with sacks of cornmeal and sugar before washing up on the porch and sitting down to eat.

When Lydia heard Mark's voice, she ran to give him a hug. "Uncle Mark, you're here. We worried you wouldn't come back to us." She squeezed him tight.

"No need to worry, sweetheart."

Lydia released her hug, then took Mark's hand, looked him in the eyes and said, "We missed you."

Mark smiled back. "If you give hugs like this all the time, you can miss me as much as you want, Lydia." Mark gently squeezed her hand and then said, "Jack's out in the barn. He'd sure appreciate some help with Ruby."

****

Sarah wondered as she had when Mark told her he needed to be away. *Did he go see Katherine Weaver?* She wouldn't ask, but if he did, *he still kept his promise and came back to help us.* Relieved to learn he was glad to be back, Sarah served Mark a steaming bowl of soup and homemade bread.

While unpacking the sacks, Sarah wondered how Mark could afford all the provisions. She asked only for medicine. "There was no cocoa powder, maple syrup, or molasses on my list, Mark. Was your sweet tooth talking to you again?"

Mark grinned.

"But I didn't give you enough money for all of this and our store credit is probably at its limit." Debt was always a worry in the back of Sarah's mind. She'd have to ask the next trip to town how much she owed. Samuel always handled the finances, now it would be up to her to take over that responsibility too.

"The extras are for the children. I paid cash for them, Sarah. And the two bags of candy you asked for are there somewhere. I know they'll want to hear about my trip to town, but I need to rest for a bit. Wake me in an hour?" Mark said as he finished his last bite of bread and headed to the barn, as the children walked in.

Sarah waited an hour and then walked to the barn to wake Mark, she didn't have the heart to disturb him. He looked peaceful, soundly asleep under the quilt she'd given him. She waited a few minutes. *He can use the rest. The children will have to save their questions until morning.*

"Where's Uncle Mark?" Jack asked when Sarah returned.

"I let him sleep. Uncle Mark needs his rest.

Tomorrow, Lydia and I will lay out the kitchen garden while you and Uncle Mark clear more land. Finish up your game of checkers and we'll all make it an early night." Sarah yawned loudly, picked up her sewing and observed as the children bantered back and forth about who would win the last game.

****

The next morning, Jack was first to come down from the loft.

"Good morning, Ma." He yawned. "What's for breakfast?"

"Flapjacks with maple syrup."

"Yea! We have maple syrup?"

Just then, Lydia bound down the ladder. "Did you say maple syrup?"

"Yes, and breakfast will be ready soon, so wash up and set the table."

Sarah listened in on the conversation as the children chatted back and forth.

Lydia jostled Jack aside and stretched to grab the plates in the cupboard behind him. "Do you think Uncle Mark brought anything for us from town?"

"Maybe. Hope so." Jack nudged her back.

"Me too. Maybe it's candy." Lydia plopped a plate on the table.

"Maybe a new deck of cards?" Jack gathered the silverware from the drawer.

At that moment, Mark walked through the door. "Someone let me sleep way past my nap last night, but I'm not complaining."

Once everyone sat down around the table, Sarah flipped the last flapjack onto a platter already piled high and Lydia offered the prayer before they dug into the special treat.

"Any new stores in town?" Lydia inquired.

Jack asked, "While you were getting the seed, did you see any new guns or knives in the cases?"

Jack and Lydia asked one question after another. Mark tried to keep up, and even when breakfast was over, they were still filled with inquiries.

"All right, time for chores," Sarah said, mid-question.

Lydia muttered, "But I didn't get to ask Uncle Mark if he brought us anything from town."

Mark looked at Sarah.

She winked back and said, "Okay, they can have them."

The children's eyes grew wide with delight.

Sarah removed two bags from the top shelf of the cupboard filled with more candy than the children ever hoped for. Lydia had hers dumped out on the table and a stick candy in her mouth before Sarah could tell them to save some for later.

"Gosh. Thanks, Uncle Mark," Jack said.

"Thank your mother," Mark said. "She's the one who asked me to get the candy for you."

"Thanks, Ma," Jack and Lydia both said. Jack gave his mother a hug.

Lydia pulled the stick candy from her mouth to give her a kiss.

Sarah licked her lips. "Mmm, peppermint," she said, and Lydia smiled.

"Look, all my favorites." Lydia started counting the pieces in her pile.

Jack offered first, "Would you like a piece of my candy?" He held out his bag to the adults.

Sarah shook her head and Mark said, "No thanks. You both enjoy it, but remember when it's gone, it's gone. So save some for a rainy day."

Mark asked Sarah to join him outside and they left the children to their bags of sweets.

Walking toward the barn, Mark said, "Sarah, the farm is doing well. Three calves were born this spring, and the hens hatched a fair number of peeps. Now if we can get the fields and the garden planted in the next few weeks, and the weather cooperates, you should be fine for the winter." He opened the barn door and they stepped into its warm darkness.

When Sarah's eyes adjusted before her sat the lumber still piled in the wagon and the sacks of seed lined up outside the milk cow's stall. Hard work lay ahead.

"Mark, I know the children enjoyed the maple syrup on their flapjacks this morning, but all the extras you bought plus the seed and lumber…you know money's tight right now and it won't be until harvest or until we can sell off a few calves this fall before there's enough money to pay you back. The store owner isn't likely to extend our credit. Somehow I'll have to pay off that debt this year too."

"Sarah, there's no need to pay me back. And you're not over extended at the general store." Mark blurted out, "I went to town to check for a letter. Last summer, a friend's brother announced he'd found a small vein of gold out west, but needed help mining it. My friend asked if I wanted to go along and if I had any money to buy supplies. I didn't want to go west at the time, so I loaned him some money so he could go help his brother.

"I never gave it much thought after that, figured I'd never see my money again. My friend and I left it that if the mine produced, he'd send word to Dead Flats this month and send me my share."

Mark took Sarah's hands in his. "The claim paid a little. I used some of my share to pay down your store bill. Please, I'm only trying to help. If Samuel were in my shoes, he'd do the same for me. The extras I bought are nothing compared to you feeding and putting up with me."

"I'm happy for you." Sarah squeezed Mark's hands, and added, "I think it's the other way around. You're putting up with us."

"Sarah, you should know," Mark continued, "I told the clerk at the hardware store about Samuel. He asked if I was new to the area, buying lumber and seed, so I explained about Samuel's accident. I'm sure by now the whole town has heard. I'm sorry I didn't ask you first before mentioning it in public, but he caught me off guard."

"No, I don't mind. I understand, Mark. That's fine. They were going to find out sooner or later."

Sarah was actually relieved to know the news of Samuel's death was out in the open. She was also comforted in a strange way to learn Mark hadn't visited Miss Katherine Weaver. *Now he probably has the money they needed to buy land, build their home, marry, and start a family.* She couldn't worry about that right now. She wasn't comfortable with Mark buying all the extras he brought home, but the biggest surprise was finding out about the gold claim.

Overwhelmed with all the news and grateful Mark returned and planned to stay and help with the planting,

Sarah pondered *he is a good, kind man and a friend to our family. He's proven he wouldn't up and leave us before the crops were planted.* Now, if he did have to leave before the harvest, at least her sister and brother were coming. Somehow she'd find a way to pay back Mark and keep Samuel's dream moving forward.

Chapter Twelve

That night after Jack and Lydia were asleep, Sarah measured the ingredients for the bread she would let rise before baking in the morning. She had an urge to talk. Mark sat at the end of the table sharpening his knife when Sara asked, "Do you mind if I bend your ear for a spell, Mark? I keep thinking about what brought our family to Kansas and I'd like to share a story."

"Of course, Sarah, go ahead." Mark continued sharpening.

Sarah poured herself and Mark a steaming cup of tea and began mixing the bread dough as she told her story about the fourteen families who set out from Pennsylvania in the spring of 1854.

"Each day our family trudged on. Our wagon train traveled only twelve to fifteen miles per day. Samuel and I had no idea what it would be like starting over and raising a family in a new location. But, we had our health, our faith, our love for each other and of course, we had our children. The promise of good farmland enticed us to make the most difficult decision of our lives.

"Samuel worked making shingles at the time and wasn't happy. He really wanted his own farm, his own land, and most of all, to be his own boss. Waving good-bye to our families wasn't easy. I'll never forget the families crying and hugging before we headed out.

Mother and the church ladies gave us a beautiful going away quilt that I cherish to this day.

"Three families from Tidioute were in the train. Others from Warren County had headed west the year before and the local letters home portrayed the journey as difficult, although well worth their efforts.

"We met up with ten other wagons before crossing into Ohio. There were to be eighteen total, but some changed their minds and a few couldn't come up with the money in time. Samuel often said, 'The excitement of the unknown is an adventure', but it turned out to be more like a nightmare at times.

"The trail master, Mr. Rohrer, made the trip to Kansas three times before. Samuel trusted his decisions, but some men argued and fistfights broke out over where to cross creeks and rivers and which towns to stop at for supplies. Thankfully, Samuel wasn't a fighter and would never use a weapon in a violent manner, two traits I loved about him.

"With the men fighting among themselves, the journey wasn't easy," Sarah said. "The women had to be strong and hold their families together, and comfort and care for the children, whether taking out a splinter or tending to a fever. I prepared a hot meal twice a day and foraged for greens, berries, and whatever else I could find along the way that was edible. There were always clothes to wash, but not always a creek close by or water to spare.

"Samuel helped as much as he could, but I couldn't always rely on him. He and the other men took turns on night watch, gathering wood and building the campfires both morning and evening, making sure the animals were cared for, and protecting our family. So, he had his own duties and worries."

"Some days were unbearably hot and the dirt and dust blew everywhere. And other times mud and water seeped into the back of the wagon when we crossed rivers and creeks. Keeping everything clean and dry was a fulltime job. I never knew what would be ruined inside the trunks. When we were on the trail, wet clothes and blankets were hung to dry on a rope strung inside the wagon and then draped over brush and tree limbs when the wagon train stopped for the night.

"I never imagined how difficult the trip would be. I sure was glad my brother Richard changed his mind to come along, although he would probably still be alive had he not come. At the time he was a God send. He helped drive the wagon, take care of the animals and other chores each day." Sarah stopped her kneading, took a sip of tea, and continued, "Samuel was constantly looking for clean water and food for the table. And keeping our team of horses and oxen fed and healthy to pull our wagon was vital to our survival. If we couldn't keep up, we'd be left behind. And of course, Samuel worried about the safety of our family with the political and Indian unrest surrounding us. There was so much to do just to survive. He was a good husband. How will we manage without him?"

Sarah closed her eyes, took a deep breath, and opened them to see Mark looking intensely at her. "You're a good friend, Mark. Thank you for staying with us," she said, and continued with her story as Mark returned to sharpening his knives with occasional glances her way.

"James and Mary Miller were three wagons back. About three weeks into the journey, crossing into

Indiana near the beginning of June, they both became ill, but insisted on continuing. James started with a twinge of stomach pain and his fever grew progressively worse. Then Mary took ill, too. The Miller's told us they had always dreamed of traveling west. We helped them until it became obvious they were too sick to continue. They only had each other. They never had children. That's why our family befriended them. My, they were stubborn.

"They didn't want to hold us up, so Samuel volunteered to stay behind and nurse them back to health. He sent the children and me on with Richard. Samuel promised they would catch up with us as soon as James' and Mary's health improved. I didn't want to leave Samuel behind, but he insisted.

"Samuel told us later he used cold compresses and wrapped the Millers in blankets to try to sweat the fever out of them, but nothing worked. James and Mary were weak and refused to eat.

"Two days after the wagon train had left, Samuel said, James died in Mary's arms. Although Samuel said he tried to get Mary to eat something to build up her strength, she refused. Samuel believed she might have lived through the night if she'd eaten, but he heard her cry out in prayer for God to take her and relieve her from her pain and grief. She just wanted to be with James.

"Now I can relate to her feelings, the same pain and grief as when you first told me about Samuel. No matter what, my first notion was to be with him. The thought of my children drew me back to reality." Sarah placed the kneaded dough in the bowl, covered it with a piece of flour sacking and set it on the hearth for the night. Back at the table, she wrapped her hands around her mug of tea and took a sip as Mark tested his knife blade for sharpness.

"Poor Mary," Sarah continued, "her physical pain, the guilt, and the grief she faced when James died must have exhausted her. She died the following day. Samuel always said he liked to think God answered her prayers.

"It was a true blessing for Mary and James to be together, but in the end the real blessing was for our family. A week prior James told Samuel, in front of some of the other men in camp and Mr. Rohrer that if they didn't make it to their land or if anything happened to both him and Mary, that Samuel was to receive all of their belongings. We didn't realize it then, but without their generous gift, our family couldn't have made it through that difficult first winter.

"Their belongings weren't the only things they gave us. When James worried he might not recover, he asked Samuel to help him write a last will and testament. It said if anything happened to him and Mary, Samuel was to keep their wagon and all their possessions including their money, to help our family set up our new home. That's how we were able to afford so much land and lumber to build.

"Samuel gave Mary and James a proper burial and caught up with us. When Samuel rode in with the Miller's wagon, we had just made camp for the night. The news spread quickly about James' and Mary's passing. Many people stopped to hear the story. Relief and a deep appreciation of security enveloped me. We were so blessed and thankful to have him returned to us safely.

"The Millers weren't the only deaths on our

journey. The Wilks's nine-year-old son, Markus, developed a fever and died. Then, an elderly man, Mr. Knox, six wagons back had heart problems. At least that's what people said. Milly Sample died giving birth to her third child and then the baby died too. My heart ached for her husband and children. Had there been a doctor, or even the proper medicine, they might have lived.

"The last person was Anne Frazer. The first months of the trip, Anne kept me from wanting to turn around and head home many times. She was a God send." A tear ran down Sarah's cheek as she remembered all the losses the traveling community endured crossing Ohio, Indiana, Illinois, Missouri, and into Kansas.

"Anne hasn't been in my thoughts for quite some time," Sarah said, tears welling in her eyes. "We were less than two weeks away from our dreams when her terrible accident occurred."

Collecting her wits, she resumed, "We rode past so many graves along the trail that I gave up counting. We'd say a prayer for each soul when we passed wooden crosses and prayed God would see fit to lead us safely to our new home.

"Some women kept track of the graves in their diaries, but the constant reminder was too dark for me. My entries were about news events, interesting finds along the trail, and things that could be shared with Lydia and Jack someday.

"Death wasn't the only sad thing that happened along the journey. There were towns we passed through in Missouri where slaves were being sold in the streets. You'd hear the women cry out for their men and children when their families were separated, whipped and sometimes shackled. Even the children witnessed torture and abuse. It's inconceivable to me how anyone condones slavery. Samuel always said the next war our country will fight will be over slaves.

"Sharing these stories remind me of so many sad memories, but there were good days too. Cheap land for emigrants that's what made the whole journey look so promising in the first place." Sarah smiled. "Our families back east are the people we really miss, my mother especially. And the tragic way my brother Richard was taken from us was so unnecessary.

"Samuel couldn't believe our luck when he found this mile-square parcel listed at the territory land grant office, in Ogden, with a quarter plot adjoining for Richard. With the stream that runs year 'round and the small grove of elm trees growing along the creek, Samuel jumped at the opportunity to look at the parcels. When we laid eyes on it, the place was perfect, better than we imagined. We'd found our new home, and because of the money the Millers left us we could afford it. Richard staked claim to his adjoining parcel the same day and we listed each other as beneficiaries if anything ever happened to us. Thank God we planned ahead.

"Three of the families from our wagon train settled in this area. The others desired to travel farther south taking the Santa Fe Trail to Oklahoma and Texas. They located a different trail master to take them and Mr. Rohrer headed back to Pennsylvania."

"The first fall we were here," Sarah continued, "the plains were in a terrible drought. With winter right around the corner, we only had time to build a temporary, one room structure with the lean-to on the back for the animals.

"Even if I swept two or three times a day, the dust would get into every crack and crevice imaginable in our first little shack. It'd get in your eyes even when they were closed. The flat dry ground of Kansas is a far cry from the lush green mountains of Pennsylvania. Although our land here in Kansas is fertile the plowing is difficult."

Sarah sipped her tea while remembering, "Then, Lydia came down with a high fever. We chanced we were going to lose her. We hadn't yet dug a well, so Samuel carried water from the creek so I could bathe her until her fever finally broke. Oh, how Samuel loved our children. Our first year was the toughest, but we made it. Now he's not here to enjoy what he helped create. My question to God every night is still, 'Why was he taken from us?'"

Sarah shook her head as though to shake off painful memories, "See that picture there on the table?" She pointed to a hand carved wooden frame sitting on a stand next to her rocking chair. "That picture made the journey in Mary Miller's trunk."

Mark walked over, picked up the picture, and was surprised when he remembered the house and the surroundings.

"That was among James' and Mary's belongings. The picture is of the house they left behind in Pennsylvania. It's there to remind me how far we've come." A tear rolled down Sarah's cheek and she quickly dabbed it away. "But it's too easy to quit. Samuel wouldn't want us to give up." She heard herself say the words and wondered if she really meant them.

****

Mark returned to his seat at the table. He'd been the friend Sarah needed tonight and hung on her every word without interruption. Now, after hearing Sarah's story, Mark leaned across the table and cupped her hands in his to comfort her. His heart was heavy with concern. He now fully understood the importance of his promises to Samuel. Sarah could care for and educate her children, manage the daily routine of the farm, and hold her family together, but who would take care of Sarah?

Chapter Thirteen

"Come on, Lydia, it's a beautiful spring day and the ground is warm enough to plant. Let's start the kitchen garden." Sarah learned from the past three years the growing season in Kansas was longer than in Pennsylvania where often only two plantings could be harvested a season. "The sooner we get it done, the sooner we can enjoy the bounty and help Mark and Jack in the fields again."

Sarah and Lydia prepared the twenty by forty foot plot which was double that of last year's garden. Emma and Matthew would arrive by fall and with the additional garden seeds Mark bought, there would be plenty of produce to harvest.

"Now, be careful to mark each row end with a twig so we know where we've planted and keep them straight and evenly spaced," Sarah reminded Lydia. She helped Lydia make a chart of the garden. Someday Lydia would plant a garden for her own family and Sarah wanted her to look back fondly on these years of learning.

"We'll plant the hardier root vegetables first like beets, carrots and parsnips," Sarah told her daughter. Then they mounded the ground in preparation to plant sweet potatoes, squash, and pumpkins. "We'll plant the rest when the weather promises to stay warm." In another week, she figured, it would be safe.

Finished for the time being, mother and daughter returned to help Mark and Jack finish the fields. Plowing and planting were hard, back breaking jobs and for another week they all pitched in. When the weather grew milder, they returned to finish planting the kitchen garden.

One rainy afternoon, Mark announced, "I have four novels. You can pick your favorite. Anyone interested?"

Glad for something new to read on such a dreary day, Lydia said, "I'll take one."

Jack spoke up, "I'd like one too."

Even Sarah indulged. "I haven't sat and read a novel in a long time."

Not much interested in reading, Mark ran through the yard jumping the mud puddles, as he headed to the barn to take a nap.

****

The following weeks everyone took turns, swapping tasks so it seemed less grueling. Sarah and Lydia exchanged tasks often, one drilling and the other dropping corn kernels. Mark and Jack cast seeds in the rye and barley fields. Lydia planted a patch of seed potatoes along the edge of a field and Sarah helped drag the fields, guiding Button with a board rigged behind to cover the seed with dirt.

One day, while working the fields, Sarah heard Jack yell, "Look, someone's coming."

As the wagon approached from the north, Sarah figured him to be Joseph Spencer. His family lived a good day's ride from the farm. Joe, his wife, Martha, and their three girls, Katy and Hannah, Jack and Lydia's age, and Grace who married last year, all journeyed west on the wagon train from Pennsylvania. Since arriving in Kansas, the two families would get together every year, meeting each other halfway between properties for a picnic in mid-October. But because of an early snowstorm last year, they weren't able to meet.

"Hello, Sarah," Joe hollered. "On my way to town and wanted to drop by and say hello." He jumped down from the wagon and took Sarah's hand in his. "Henry and Hilda Huber stopped in March and told us about the loss of your child. This is the first chance I've had to get to town since. We were unable to visit then because our Katy took ill with a fever. Martha was so grieved when she heard of your loss. You doing all right now?"

"Yes, Joe. Thanks for your concern. It's nice of you to stop and visit." Sarah's eyes moistened, as the thought of recalling the two worst events in her life overwhelmed her. First chills prickled her skin and then a burst of warmth penetrated her body.

"I'm heading to town to pick up more seed. After last winter, I'm not taking a chance of losing any more animals. It looks like Samuel did the same. The fields look great." Joe looked at the man approaching. "Why that's not Samuel. He looks like Mark Hewitt? Why, what's he doing here? It's been years since we've talked. And where's Samuel today?"

Sarah dreaded this moment having to share with others about Samuel's demise. As Mark approached, she crossed her arms and held herself, then answered, "Yes, Mark Hewitt, Samuel's good friend is here visiting with us."

Hearing Sarah's voice quiver, Mark picked up his pace, walked over, and shook Joe's hand, leading him aside to explain what happened to Samuel.

Joe's head dropped to his chest and shook in disbelief. "I feel terrible for Sarah and the children losing Samuel to an accident. Sarah's lucky to have you staying on."

Mark explained he would be staying at least until the crops were planted and Sarah's siblings arrived from Pennsylvania to stay with her.

Mark called, "Children, come over and greet Mr. Spencer before he heads to town."

The children said their hellos with Lydia sending a message to her friends that she hoped to see them this summer.

Sarah and Joe exchanged a hug. "If there's anything Martha and I can do for you, Sarah, get word to us. Would you like to get together for our annual picnic again this October? I know how you gals like to catch up on things and get together to swap fabric for quilt patches."

"I'd like that." Sarah nodded.

"Oh, and Martha wanted you to know Grace had her baby a few months back. Can you believe we are grandparents already?"

This news made Sarah brighten and smile. "A boy or a girl?"

"A little girl, Rebecca June, and she's doing well."

Sarah's smile grew wider, "Well congratulation, Grandpa. Tell Martha we have lots to catch up on our next visit." Then her thoughts turned to Samuel. *sweetheart, I'm so sorry you'll never get to hold or enjoy our grandchildren.*

"Do you think you'll make it into town for the Fourth of July Celebration or the Fall Harvest Festival this year?" Joe inquired.

"At this point, I'm not sure." Sarah again clutched her arms to her body fearful she might collapse if she didn't. "We'll have to see how the planting goes."

Joe stepped up into his wagon and Mark whispered, "We'll be all right."

As they all waved good-bye and returned to their tasks, Sarah strained to call to Joe, "Make sure you tell Martha and the girls we said hello." *It's good to see a friendly face, if only the circumstances were different.*

That evening, after the children were in bed, Sarah said to Mark. "It was nice of Joe to stop and share his family's condolences for Baby Walter. Thanks for stepping in and explaining about Samuel."

"No problem. I hadn't seen him in quite some time. We went to school and later worked odd jobs together. Samuel mentioned they joined the wagon train, but I didn't realize he lived so close."

"Yes, Martha and I did many baskets of wash at the creek, standing beside each other, on the journey to Kansas. Their two youngest girls are good friends with Jack and Lydia."

****

The planting continued even on Sundays knowing the good Lord would be forgiving. At the end of each day, accomplishment reigned over them as they washed off the dust and dirt of the day's activities, ate supper, and dragged their tired bodies to bed early each night.

One night, after the children were in bed, while Sarah washed the supper dishes and Mark dried, she explained, "I can't thank you enough, Mark, for staying and helping us get the fields cleared and planted. We'd still be plowing and planting for months toiling by ourselves before we finished."

"My pleasure, Sarah."

"Now when Emma and Matthew arrive, we'll be all set. Samuel checked last fall, while in town, and Mr. Rohrer is still organizing wagon trains in Pennsylvania. Mother has written several times and assures me the money is available. Funny, I have this nagging feeling. What if they can't come this year? Would it be imposing too much if I asked you to take us to town? There should be a letter from my mother waiting at the postal office. I have to know if my brother and sister are on their way."

"Of course I'll take you, Sarah."

"Thanks, Mark. We could make it a special celebration and go for the Fourth of July Festival coming up in a few weeks."

"Why, that sounds like a good idea. I'm sure Jack and Lydia would welcome the break. Some fun would do them good. They've been a great help and worked hard." Mark finished drying the last dish and placed it in the cupboard.

"Sometime soon, could you ride over and see if Seth Frazer could come feed the livestock while we're away?"

The name Frazer. Mark heard Sarah say the name Frazer before, but couldn't place it.

"Of course, I wasn't thinking about the livestock. Daisy can't be left alone two nights or she'll dry up." Now he remembered the name. Seth's wife, Anne, died on the way to Kansas.

"Jack and I'll ride over to Seth's place tomorrow morning," Mark said.

That evening, Sarah brewed some spearmint tea

she grew and dried. "Come sit awhile, Mark, and relax without the children demanding your time." Sitting across from each other, they talked about the children and planned the trip to town, realizing only when the regulator clock on the wall chimed eleven the new day would start in an hour.

"We'll have to do this again." Sarah missed talking with Samuel this way and was glad to have Mark there to help out.

"I agree. Thank you for the tea, Sarah." Mark took his teacup to the sink and headed to the door, then stopped as Sarah bent to blow out the flame of the table lamp.

Sarah noticed Mark gazing at her. "Is something wrong?"

Mark hesitated, wanting to look at her one more time before heading to the barn. *What were these feelings welling up inside him? Could he be falling in love with Sarah or had he always loved her? But this wasn't the right time. Not enough time passed since Samuel's death*, so he shook his head, "No, everything's good." He walked across the moonlit yard to his bed in the barn. Although later than usual after their talk, he couldn't sleep. His mind already drifted back to his feelings for Sarah.

****

At breakfast, Sarah asked Jack, "Think you can help Mark find Mr. Frazer's place?"

"Sure I can, Ma. I rode there with Pa many times. It takes about three hours to get there."

After chores, Sarah gave Mark the crock of last night's stew and packed cornbread muffins for their trip plus two loaves of pumpkin bread, hot out of the oven fresh, for Seth.

"You ready, Jack?"

"Yup, I'm ready." Jack swung up onto his poppa's horse, Button, and sat proud in the saddle. Mark let Jack take the lead and they waved good-bye as they rounded the first bend in the creek heading west.

It didn't take Jack long before he started talking. "You don't know Mr. Frazer do you Mark?"

"No, we've never met."

"Seth and his wife Anne lived in Sheffield, back home, right over the mountain from Tidioute where we lived. The Frazer's had just married when they joined the wagon train. They came west because of the promise of good land and a prosperous life, like Ma and Pa.

"We'll have to cross this winding creek four times before we get to Mr. Frazer's place. You'll like Mr. Frazer. He's a nice man, but I think he's lonely."

"Why's that, Jack?"

"His wife died and he never remarried. The accident happened fording one of the rivers to get here. The horses were halfway across when they lurched forward and she was caught off guard. She fell into the water and got trapped under the wagon and drowned. Pa said Seth blamed himself for her death. He can't get over it because he drove the wagon when it happened."

"Were your mother and Mrs. Frazer good friends?"

"Oh, yes. On the trail they would cook meals and do wash at the creek together. Ma told Lydia and me if Mrs. Frazer told us to do something, it was as good as if she said it herself. We were to mind Mrs. Frazer like we minded Ma."

"Do you know if your father and Seth were good

friends too?"

"Not like Mrs. Frazer and Ma, although they did things to help each other. Mr. Frazer comes over and feeds the animals for us when we go to town and last year he helped us with the harvest a few days. Pa picks up supplies for him in town, sometimes, saving him the long trip. Hey, we could offer to help him out if he needs anything in town," Jack said, proud of himself for thinking like his poppa.

"Sure we could do that."

Time passed as they rode across the prairie grass waving in the breeze, comfortable in the heat of mid-morning. They crossed the creek again.

"How much farther, Jack? This is the third time we've crossed the creek." Mark wiped his brow.

"Right up ahead are some shade trees. Pa and I always took a break there and ate a bite. Then it's only a short distance."

"Good, I'm getting hungry. How about you?

"Me too." Jack smiled, knowing he got them to this place without getting lost. His poppa would be proud of him.

At the shade trees beside the creek they stopped and rested the horses, letting them drink in the cool stream and graze.

"Pa always seemed in a hurry to get to Mr. Frazer's place. Then we'd spend an hour or so catching up on news, which bored me. Then we'd turn around and head home."

Mark and Jack ate the leftover stew and one muffin each, saving the other muffin for the ride back home. Refreshed, they rode through the grass until in the distance sat Seth Frazer's place.

The homestead wasn't what Mark expected. The house was a small log structure with a chimney, one window, an overhang above the door and a wooden stoop. The barn was another small log structure with a lean-to and hen house attached.

Jack yelled out, "Mr. Frazer! Are you home? It's me, Jack Clark, and this here's a friend of my pa's, Mark Hewitt! Are you here? He started leading his horse toward the house.

Mr. Frazer slowly opened the door and poked his head out. "Is that you yelling, Jack?" he asked.

"Yes sir. It's me."

Startled by the fact Samuel wasn't with his son. Seth said, "That's Samuel's horse, so who are you and where's Samuel?"

"My name is Mark Hewitt and I'm a good friend of Samuel's."

"Is he coming too?" Seth asked.

"I have some things to tell you, Seth. But first, Jack, do you think you could take the horses, tie them up in the shade, and give them some water?"

"All right, and then I'll come in."

"C'mon inside." Seth motioned for Mark to sit at the table.

Mark couldn't help notice Seth hadn't shaved in months and his hair was long and stringy. His hands looked rough and calloused. Mark figured him for a hard worker.

As he sat on the bench and rested his arms on the table, Mark said, "I've some bad news about Samuel, and I'd rather Jack not hear our conversation. He already knows the details. Samuel and I were hunting up by Blue Rapids and shot a deer for some fresh meat.

Mark finished his now familiar fabricated story and hung his head in sorrow.

"Poor Sarah." Seth shook his head.

"I was with Samuel when he died. I promised him I'd take care of his family. I grew up with him and we promised each other we'd watch out for the other if anything ever happened.

"We cleared more land and the crops are planted. Now Sarah would like to go to town to see if there's any word about her brother and sister coming to live with her this fall," Mark said.

Seth stood and paced the floor. "Sorry to hear about Samuel. How is Sarah dealing with all of this and the new baby?"

"When was the last you talked to the family?" Mark asked.

"Last September I visited, before the family attended the Fall Festival. Sarah was so excited about having their third child." Seth sat back down at the table.

"Seth, I'm sorry to tell you, but the baby died in January. Sarah was devastated afterward. Samuel and the children had a hard time dealing with the loss too."

Jack stepped through the door, held out the pumpkin bread he'd fetched from Mark's saddlebag, and gave it to Seth. "This is for you from Ma, Mr. Frazer. Sorry introductions were short."

"That's okay, Jack," Seth muttered. "Since he's with you, I figured he was all right."

"He's more than all right, Mr. Frazer. He's my pa's best friend. He's been helping our family since my pa died. Did you tell him, Mark?"

"Yes, everything." Mark nodded.

"Can you help us out and come feed the animals for us when we go to town, Mr. Frazer?" Jack asked.

"Sure can, Jack. There's nothing here that can't be put on hold for a couple of days."

"Don't you have any livestock?" Mark asked.

"The five steers will be fine in the pasture and the chickens can have extra chop. They'll be fine." Seth pointed to the calendar. "What day are you leaving?"

"We'll leave on July 3rd after morning chores," Mark answered.

"Sounds good. I'll be there that evening and sleep in the barn like I did before. Now where are my manners?" Seth said. "Would you like a slice of your mother's bread, Jack, after riding all that way?"

"Sure, but only a thin slice please. Ma made it special for you. Oh, and she told me to ask you if you'd like a cake or a pie when you come to feed the animals and to tell you she'd have a cooked chicken and leftovers for you wrapped in the root cellar. You're to help yourself," Jack said.

"That's mighty nice of her," Seth said, then turned to Jack and asked, "What day did you say today was?"

"Today's Thursday, June 18th."

Seth glanced at his calendar hanging on the wall and said, "I must have missed a few days here and there. It seemed a little warm for May 29th," which was the last day crossed off his calendar. He made a big X over June 18th, and then sliced some pumpkin bread for everyone. Using small china plates, trying to be hospitable, he carried them to the table.

"Sorry there isn't anything to go with the bread, but the coffee bin is empty and sugar is scarce. Town's too far to get to very often, but there's not much to need around here." Seth said, looking around his house.

Besides the table and four chairs in the middle of the cabin, there wasn't much else. A pegged coat rack hung by the door and a stand with shelves and some crocks stood beside a dry sink. There was a fireplace with a nice deep hearth, a few pots and pans on the floor, and in one corner a bed with blankets muddled. Seth changed the subject saying, "The fields are plowed and planted, but I'll have to get my garden planted."

"I'm sure Ma has some extra seed leftover from her garden. I know we have pumpkin and squash seed. We'll leave it on the kitchen table for you. No reason letting them go to waste," Jack said.

"Is there anything you'd like us to pick up for you while we're in town?" Jack asked, like he heard his poppa do many times.

"Come to think of it, fifty pounds of corn meal, and twenty-five each of coffee, sugar, and salt would set me for a while. Oh, and two tins of gunpowder. You sure you don't mind?"

"Mind, no. Glad to help out, Seth," Mark said.

"Let me get you some money." Seth grabbed a crock from the self and took out three silver dollars and two silver quarters. Will this cover it?" He asked.

"Sure will," Mark said, then looked at Jack, "We best be on our way. Your mother is expecting us home in time for supper."

"Tell your mother thanks for the pumpkin bread and a cake sure will taste good." Seth smiled.

Everyone walked outside. Mark shook Seth's hand. "Nice meeting you, Seth, and many thanks for agreeing to take care of the livestock."

As Mark and Jack mounted the horses, Seth said,

"Nice meeting you too. Sure glad to help if it means one of Sarah's cakes. I'll be over to pick up those supplies someday after you're back."

Mark nodded and Jack and Mark waved good-bye and were off again, this time heading east.

Chapter Fourteen

Thursday morning everyone helped pack the wagon for the trip to town. Sarah called out, "Don't forget your swimming clothes." She heard Lydia yell up the loft, 'Jack, I told you to pack swimming clothes.'"

"Since you're packed, Lydia, please gather the eggs for me to sell in town," Sarah said as she handed her the egg basket. The sale would add a little to Sarah's money jar.

Mark stuck his head in the door and called out, "Come on, let's get going. "If we leave now, we'll get a few hours of travel in before the sun gets too blooming hot."

"Are you entering the Annual Best Shot Contest, Uncle Mark?" Jack asked, climbing down the ladder from the loft, his clothes bundled and ready to travel.

"I didn't know Dead Flats held one every year."

"Poppa entered every time. He came close a couple times, but never won. The town has contests twice a year, once on the Fourth of July and again at the Fall Festival. We mainly get to go only to the Fall Festival because we're usually too busy around here to leave over the Fourth of July."

"Well, I just might enter, Jack," Mark said, heading for the barn.

Jack called out, "Please grab the fishing poles

when you get your Sharps rifle."

"Come on, children, hurry." Sarah called out one last time as she finished packing the wagon, carefully placing her baked goods in the tiered wooden holder wedged between two sacks of oats for the horses. There were three loaves of pumpkin bread and two pumpkin pies along with a gallon crock filled with pickled eggs to share at the picnic. Last night, Sarah got an urge to try her hand at the pie contest. Using the last of the molasses, she made her favorite wet bottom shoe-fly pie, a traditional Pennsylvania recipe. The main stay for the rest of their meals were fresh vegetables picked from the garden that morning to snack on, a pot of stew, muffins, and a crock of mint tea.

"We're ready to leave. Come on, Mark. Let's get going."

Jack took the reins and Mark rode his horse so the children could sit on the wagon's bench seat with their mother. A canopy rigged in the back of the spring wagon offered shade.

Sarah's plan was they were going to town to mail her letter and check on word from her family. There wasn't money enough for anything else, but they would stay the night in the church grove with others from out of town and join in the Fourth of July celebration and town picnic. It would be good for the children to see their friends.

Once underway, the children talked with excitement about the adventure to town. Lydia packed the new skirt she made. "I can't wait to go to the dry goods store to see the fabrics. Do you think after the harvest we'll have money enough for some cloth, Ma?"

"We'll see, dear." Sarah couldn't promise that far

in advance.

"I can't wait to see the guns and knives in the cabinet at the hardware store. Someday I'll have my own gun so I can go hunting and provide for our family." Jack puffed out his chest. "Mark, would you teach me how to shoot? Pa didn't take me hunting much, but we did plenty of fishing together. We caught our share of fish, didn't we, Ma?"

"Yes, you and your father loved fishing." Sarah smiled.

"Of course I'll teach you how to shoot and hunt, Jack." Mark grinned, pleased Jack had asked him.

They stopped for a light picnic meal and enjoyed applesauce on the biscuits Sarah made fresh that morning and a crock of sweet raspberry juice cooled their thirst on the hot afternoon. Feeling the heat and seeing the dust kicked up from the horses' hooves reminded Sarah of the long wagon ride from Pennsylvania. She told a familiar story about the trip, then Jack shared one, then Lydia. The stories made time pass quickly.

Sarah told about some of the meals she cooked and then said, "I never made so many different kinds of biscuits in my life with all the berries and wild herbs we found crossing the different states. Samuel enjoyed a different flavor with his coffee all the time.

Jack told a story about fishing with his poppa one night along a creek where they camped. "I caught a fish every time I dropped my line. Pa never got his line wet. He said he was too busy looking for bait for my hook. I think I caught six or seven. Do you remember, Ma?"

"I sure do. We had pan fried fish that night for dinner and your father loved it."

Lydia rubbed her hands together as she told her story about burning herself. "Since the fire was out, I figured the left over pieces of wood wouldn't be hot. They didn't look hot, but I quickly learned white ash doesn't mean they can't burn you. What a surprise. I had to wear a cloth bandage around my hand for a couple of weeks. It really hurt. Luckily Ma knew what to do and applied lard to it right away."

"I remember," Jack said, "because you couldn't get your hand wet and I had to wash and dry all the dishes."

When they arrived at the old oak tree campsite in the early evening, where the family always camped when they traveled to town, the clouds finally covered the sun to provide relief. The family always camped at this spot. Samuel and Mark had stopped here on their first trip back from town. Before arriving at Dead Flats tomorrow, they would still have a four-hour wagon ride.

Once camp was in order, Jack braved the question with sweat beading on his cheeks, "Can we go swimming before supper? Please, Ma. We're old enough to go by ourselves this year."

The sun is hot and we've been in the wagon for such a long time. A refreshing dip in the creek would certainly feel good. Both children are good swimmers, but if anything happened... Sarah wasn't ready to let them go alone. "Mark has never seen you do your tricks underwater. Why don't we come along? Do you mind Mark?"

"Sounds good. I might even join in." Mark understood Sarah's concern.

"Okay, we can show him how we walk on our hands in the water and how long we can hold our breath, Lydia." Jack jumped in the air, 'Wah who,' and ran to change clothes.

Lydia wore an old top tucked into the bloomers she made special for swimming. Jack wore an old pair of cotton pants, cut off at the knees.

"I'll race you to the swimming hole." Jack challenged.

Lydia couldn't keep up and Jack jumped in first.

"Come on in or I'll splash you." Jack skimmed his hand along the top of the water.

Lydia giggled and jumped in, her hazel eyes filled with delight as the sun glistened on the water.

The children swam and played while Sarah spread an old quilt on the grassy bank and invited Mark to sit and join her.

"Watch this, Uncle Mark. Look how easy I can walk on my hands." Jack dunked under water with his feet sticking straight up, and slowly crossed the swimming hole. At its deepest, the water was about five feet and the creek was more than twice that across, but it changed every year depending on rainfall.

Not to be outdone by her brother, Lydia followed with her feet skimming the surface.

After coming up for air, Jack asked, "Do you want to play the rock game, Lydia?"

"Sure. Look there's one with a notch that'll be perfect. It'll be easy to find." Lydia plunged to the bottom to pick it from the creek's bed.

"Uncle Mark, here's how we play. One person drops the rock, the other person has to dive down, find it, and hold it up. Whoever finds it the fastest gets the point."

"You can go first, Lydia." Jack dropped the stone.

"Ma, will you be the counter and decide who wins?"

"Sure."

Lydia dunked under water and found the rock on the first dive. The count was five seconds. Both children dove several times for the rock, having a good time taking turns. The last time Jack dropped the rock, the current caught it on the way down and carried it close to the creek bank, right in front of Sarah and Mark.

"I can get it," Lydia said as she dunked into the water to search.

Sarah started counting, but when she got to eight and Lydia hadn't come up, Jack looked and yelled, "Ma, Lydia's stuck. She can't get loose."

Mark jumped into the water. Lydia's long hair was wrapped around a tree root preventing her from surfacing. He grabbed his pocketknife and cut Lydia's hair, not an easy task. Finally, he lifted her out of the water, cradling her limp body in his arms. He hoisted her onto the creek bank and quickly checked for breathing and a heartbeat.

Mark shook her, "Lydia, can you hear me? Can you open your eyes?" He brushed strands of hair away from her face and placed a hand on her chest to check for breathing. Sarah, frantic, tried to check Lydia's limp wrist for a pulse. Mark shook Lydia again, then pressed firmly on her chest a few times to force her to start breathing. Finally, Lydia opened her eyes and began coughing and gasping for breath. Mark turned her on her side and Sarah patted her back until she coughed out water. Once breathing normally, Mark sat her upright, holding her shoulders to steady her.

Sarah cried out, "Is she all right? Is my baby all

right?" Then it dawned on her, if she were alone with the children, she wouldn't have had a knife to save her daughter's life.

Jack knelt by Lydia's side. "This was my fault. I'm sorry, Lydia, for dropping the rock so close to the bank. Don't be mad at me." Tears filled his eyes.

"I'm not mad at you, Jack." Dazed by what happened. Lydia tried to stand, but her head was disoriented. She clung to Mark who lifted her away from the edge of the water and placed her gently on the quilt.

After a moment or two, Lydia said, "I'm good now. I was scared, Ma. I held my breath as long as I could. I couldn't get my hair untangled. I tried, but I couldn't get free. Then I don't remember what happened."

"I'm so sorry, Lydia. It's my fault, Ma." Jack wiped his eyes.

"It's not your fault, Jack." Lydia took his hand and squeezed.

"It's really no one's fault, it just happened," Sarah said as she brushed Lydia's shorn locks back from her face, put her arms around her daughter's shoulders and held her tight. Looking up at Mark, she mouthed the words, "Thank you."

Mark nodded once and smiled.

"No, really, I'm good." Lydia smiled, pulling back from her momma's embrace. Then she touched her hair. "But Ma, my hair, It's uneven and ugly. The kids in town will make fun of me."

"I'll trim it and it will look fine." Sarah reassured her, "The important thing is you're safe."

"I think we've done enough swimming for today,"

Mark said. "Hey, I'm getting hungry. Anyone else hungry?"

"I'm counting on a couple of fresh fish for supper," Sarah announced. "You fellows grab your poles and get busy catching some dinner. Lydia and I will get a fire started."

Once there were glowing coals and the potatoes were cooking, Sarah evened out Lydia's hair with Mark's straight edged razor. "There, I'm finished," she said, after a while.

Lydia touched her shorn locks with her hands. "It's shorter, but hair always grows back."

****

After enjoying a meal of fresh fish, Mark told them all a fishing story while the fire died down. "One day, when your father and I were about your age, Jack, we tried to out fish each other before it got dark.

"Your father took one side of the stream and I took the other. The fish were biting and we fished until we couldn't see the tips of our fishing poles. By the time we finally gave up, the night sky was pitch black. We were lucky to find the trail back to town. We told fish stories all the way home. When we got to your father's house, we counted the fish in each other's sacks. It turned out Samuel caught one fish more than me, so he won the bet, although I think mine were bigger." Mark chuckled.

Jack asked, "What was the bet?"

"The loser had to give three fish to the winner leaving me four to take home. I remember my mother fried them for dinner after she scolded me for being out so late.

When the story ended, Jack wished he had a friend

to go fishing with and someone other than just Lydia to talk to and play games with.

"Okay, story time is over. It's time for bed," Sarah said.

"It's late and we want to get an early start." Mark reminded them. The weather was warm, so they didn't need a fire, only light blankets.

Lydia gave Mark a hug goodnight. "Thanks for saving me," she whispered in his ear.

"You're very welcome," Mark whispered back. "You have a very special place in my heart and I never want to see you hurt. Now go get some sleep." He kissed her forehead.

Lydia and Sarah slept in the back of the wagon and Jack and Mark crawled under it with their blankets.

"Uncle Mark," Jack whispered. "You saved Lydia's life today. I'm glad you were here." A tear ran down his cheek.

"I'm glad I was here, too, Jack. But it really wasn't your fault. Don't blame yourself."

"I know."

"Then let's get some sleep," Mark whispered back, and settled in for the night.

****

The sun broke the horizon with welcoming brightness and warmth. After a breakfast of steaming hot grits, Sarah and Lydia loaded the camping supplies while Jack and Mark hitched up the wagon.

As Lydia looked at her reflection in the creek, she caught Mark glancing her way. Self-conscious of her uneven hair, she didn't say anything because she didn't want Mark or Jack to feel bad. After all, Momma was right. It wasn't anyone's fault. Her hair would grow back in time.

"Is everyone ready to head to town? Four hours to get there, so we best be going," Lydia heard her momma say.

Lydia crawled up into the back of the wagon and sat on a blanket to soften the bumps. "Know any songs, Uncle Mark?" she asked.

"I think I can come up with a few." He started singing "Camp Town Races" and everyone joined in to help carry the tune. Time passed while they sang songs and looked for wildlife along the way.

****

Later, after the singing died down and the children were entertaining themselves playing a game of cards in the back of the wagon, Sarah had time to think about the family going to a public gathering for the first time since Samuel's death. She wasn't sure how she would handle questions about Mark. Someone was bound to make a comment.

"Mark, the question about you staying at the farm is bound to come up in conversation while we're in town. I plan to tell folks you stayed on to help with the crops."

"Well, it is the truth." Mark took off his hat and ran his figures through his hair. "I can't argue with that."

"Yes, being truthful is important," Sarah agreed. "If people think my family is alone at the farm, they may try to take advantage of the situation, especially since we live so far away from town."

Chapter Fifteen

Two miles outside of town, Mark asked Jack, "Can you handle the wagon and get the family to town all right?"

"Sure, I can."

Mark looked at Jack and winked.

"He's up to something. I know he's up to something," Jack said, as he winked back.

"I'll meet you in front of the dry goods store." Mark tipped his hat and galloped off, riding ahead to town.

At the store, Mark selected a blue bonnet with a lace ruffle to match Lydia's new outfit made from the fabric her poppa chose for her on one of his last trips to town. The bonnet would help hide her shorn locks and be the perfect addition to her outfit.

Waiting on the wooden walkway, Mark greeted the Clark family, "You made it," he said, although he wasn't surprised. Jack was good with the horses and handled the wagon just fine.

Mark stood with both hands behind his back, obviously hiding something. Lydia jumped from the wagon trying to get a peek. Then when she couldn't wait any longer, she asked, "What's behind your back, Uncle Mark?"

Mark took a step back, bowed to Lydia's level and held out the bonnet, "This is for you Lydia, to go with your new outfit."

"I love it. Come on, let's go inside so I can look in the big mirror." She motioned for them to follow.

Sarah grabbed the eggs and everyone walked inside.

"Sweetheart, you look beautiful," Sarah said, as Lydia twirled in front of the mirror.

While Jack and Mark were admiring Lydia's new bonnet, Sarah explained to the storeowner, "We'll have to buy a few extras and put it on our bill today, but our crops are planted and we have high hopes for a good season. I'm sure I'll be able to pay off our debt after the harvest.

The heavy-set man looked at his logbook and said, "Samuel's friend"—pointing to Mark—"made a payment when he was in last, Mrs. Clark. It's no problem for you to charge today. My records show you are Paid-in-Full."

Sarah was surprised at first to hear the words Paid-in-Full. *Of course, he wouldn't say anything. He's a gentleman. I bet he used some of his gold money.* She lifted her basket to the counter and sold her eggs.

Mark flipped a three-cent piece, to Jack and another to Lydia. "Here, you can each pick out some candy and maybe buy a new pair of laces for your shoes."

Mark grinned as the children peered through the glass, eye's bulging at the tempting array of root beer barrels, stick candy, molasses and caramel squares, and licorice strings.

After the supplies Seth Frazer had requested were placed in the wagon, they drove to the church grove where they would spend the night. Mark unhitched the horses and walked them to the creek for a drink while Jack and Lydia gathered firewood for later, placing it under the wagon behind the right wheel to keep it dry if it rained like they had done so many times on the wagon trip west.

Mark and the children made a quick stop at the bank where Jack and Lydia waited outside while Mark made a small withdrawal from the reward money account. Then they headed to the stables to see the horses and cattle. Sarah walked to the postal office to check for a letter from her family.

****

Sarah greeted Postmaster Foster with a smile.

He returned with a letter in his hand, "I was so sorry to hear about your husband, Mrs. Clark. Samuel was a good man."

Sarah nodded and politely said, "Thank you." Finding a place for privacy, she opened the letter from her mother.

May 8, 1858

Tidioute, Warren Co., PA

Dearest Sarah,

We were very saddened to receive your letter informing us of Samuel's death. My heart aches for you, Sarah. Words alone cannot express my sorrow for your loss. God's will is never easy to understand when it takes away someone we love. Trust in God's word that you will meet again. Your love for Samuel ran deep. If only we lived closer so I could be there to support and comfort you in your times of need. I love and miss you and the children very much.

I did as you asked and went in person to see Samuel's mother Polly to tell her of her son's death and explain the details as you wrote them. She was comforted to know you and the children were all right. She told me she knew when I pull up in the buggy that it had to be bad news. We visited all day. I hoped to see Samuel's sister, but Victoria did not come home before I left. Polly took the news of her son's death as well as could be expected. She told me she would seek peace reading from the family Bible.

My heart also aches for Polly. I ached the same way after hearing of Richard's death, so I know how she is feeling. She has visited once since that day I told her about Samuel and seems to be accepting her loss. Please write to her soon and tell her about the children. She would love to hear from you.

Sarah agreed after reading the back of the first page. *Yes, Mother is right. I must write Samuel's Mother today. I'll tell her about her grandchildren to give some peace to her heart.*

I have some news to share with you, my darling Sarah, about your father. He took ill very suddenly. The Doc says it's his heart. He had a spell. It was touch and go for a while. We almost lost him. The Doc says he will be all right, but it will take time before he can return to work. Doc also says he should take it easy and not lift heavy things or work too hard or it could occur again. He sure gave us all a scare.

Sarah's eyes filled with tears. She composed herself and read on.

Because of your father's weak heart, your brother and sister decided to stay here in Pennsylvania and will not make the trip to Kansas this summer. They do not want to leave when their father needs their help here. I am glad for them to stay on. I do hope you understand.

I would have sent Emma by herself, but I am too fearful of her traveling alone with the political unrest in our county right now. Matthew said to tell you he will come next year.

I so wish you were here. Have you thought about returning now that Samuel is gone? Whatever your decision, I will be here for you, but promise me if you cannot manage you will return east. You and the children are always welcome.

Sarah turned the page.

Of course, I understand Mother. I couldn't have left you and Father at a time like this either. They're doing the right thing. Jack and Lydia will be disappointed, but they'll get over it.

She read on.

I was relieved to hear Samuel's friend Mark stayed on to help you get the crops planted and hope he will be able to help with the harvest since Matthew will not be coming. I am sure Jack is helping too, but at age twelve I would think he is much too young to manage the heavy labor required in planting the fields himself.

I think of you and the children often and pray everything is going well. I am sure Jack has grown into a handsome young man and by now Lydia is a beautiful young lady much different from my memories of a little girl twirling her long red curls and a wiry boy who couldn't sit still. It seems so much longer than four years since you left. I miss you all very much.

Sarah, you and the children can always come back home if times get too hard or money too tight. News of political unrest between anti- and pro-slavery activities in Kansas are printed in our newspapers. I pray for your safety and worry about the territory you live in with the Potawatomi Indians so close. Please write and let us know you are safe and whether you are considering returning east.

Prayers and blessings,
Mother

She read the letter again. Her heart heavy with fear, her stomach churning into knots trying to come to terms with her father's health. She contemplated her new situation with her sister and brother not coming. Tear drops fell from her cheeks. There was a silent unspoken understanding when the wagon train left Pennsylvania that she and her parents probably would never see each other again. Now, with her father's health at risk, it dawned on her that possibility might come true. She probably wouldn't see her parents again. The realization hit her hard. She placed her hand to her lips and said a prayer for her father's recovery.

Composing herself again, Sarah put her mother's letter in her pocket and walked to the general store where she told the owner's wife, "I would like to purchase four sheets of paper, two envelopes, a bottle of ink, and a pen, please. I need to write two letters and get them in the mail today."

"Of course," the woman said when a tear trickled down Sarah's cheek. "Is everything all right, dear?"

Another tear escaped. "I just received some bad news. My father's health is not good and I need to write my mother immediately," Sarah confided, needing to tell someone.

"No problem, my dear, you come back here and sit down. Take as much time as you need," the woman said. "Here, you can use my stationery, pen, and ink."

"Please let me pay you for the supplies," Sarah

insisted.

"I won't hear of it," the woman told her.

"Thank you. I appreciate your kindness," Sarah said, tears clouding her eyes. Then as she struggled to find the right words, she quickly penned a letter straight from her heart.

July 4, 1858

Dearest Mother,

I am so sorry to hear of Father's illness. It must have really given you a scare. I was glad to learn he will recover over time. Please tell Father, I love him and wish him well very soon. You know I have missed you, Father and my siblings terribly since I left. I always dreamed perhaps I would return home someday to see you and Father again, but I realize that will probably never happen.

Please know the children and I are fine. Mark has insisted he stay on to help for a while. No need to worry about us. We have planted a fine kitchen garden for a large crop since we expected Matthew and Emma would be coming to stay. Weather permitting, of course, we will have a wonderful harvest. With Mark's help we also cleared and planted more land for feed for the cattle.

As much as my heart aches to see you all, Mother, I truly believe we should stay here in Kansas for now. The children love our home and have told me they would like to keep their father's dream alive working the farm and raising cattle.

We were so looking forward to Emma and Matthew's arrival, but they made the right decision to stay with you and Father in Pennsylvania. Tell Father I will pray for his full recovery. You are always in my prayers.

Take care of yourself, Mother, and write when you can.

Your loving daughter,
Sarah

Palms damp and feeling sadness welling up inside her, Sarah started to pen another letter to her mother-in-law, Polly. She forced herself to take a deep breath and started the letter, knowing if she wrote it now, it could be mailed this trip.

July 4, 1858

Dear Mother Clark,

I am so sorry I have not written sooner. Mother wrote that she told you the news in person of our Samuel's death. I still can't believe he is gone. I miss him terribly. I hope you find comfort in God's grace.

I want you to know we buried Baby Walter in the same coffin with Samuel. I placed our tiny baby in Samuel's arms myself. As my mother explained, Baby Walter died in January and because the ground was frozen, only a shallow grave was dug. When Mark Hewitt, Samuel's friend from Pennsylvania dug Samuel's grave, he removed Walter's tiny coffin and dug the hole larger. I am at peace knowing they rest together.

The children and I are fine and our health is good. Thankfully, Mark was here when Samuel passed and is staying to help with the crops. We planted a fine garden. Weather permitting, we will have a full root cellar this year. We have eight head of cattle, including three new calves born this spring. Working the land together helps keep Samuel's dream alive.

Sarah heard the town clock chime eleven and quickly finished.

Would you please consider visiting my mother? I am sure she would love to see you. I worry about both of you and think of you often.

You would not believe how much the children have grown in the past four years. We all miss you and would enjoy hearing from you. Please write and let us know how you and Victoria are doing.

With all my love,

Sarah,

She thanked the owner's wife and rushed to mail her letters. She paid the Postmaster from her egg money and walked toward the east end of town in search of the children and Mark.

****

Meanwhile, Mark complimented Lydia on the ruffled skirt she made herself and her new bonnet trying to make her forget about her unevenly shorn hair. Mark could tell Lydia wasn't much interested in the cattle, but just by the way her skirt swished back and forth as she walked through town Mark could tell she enjoyed showing off her new outfit.

Arriving at the stables, Lydia spied a litter of kittens and used a piece of straw to play with them. Mark looked around to make sure she was safe, then called to her, "Don't leave the stables, Lydia." and turned his attention to the cattle pens.

"Well, which of these three-year olds look good to you, Jack?" Mark asked as Jack jumped up on the corral fence to get a better vantage point.

"Pa taught me to always look for a strong back. They also have to have clear eyes. Pa wouldn't buy them if they had any cuts or infections, so we always checked the legs and hoofs and the nose and mouth to make sure they were healthy."

"Your father taught you well, Jack."

Mark looked over the herd for a mother with a calf that met all of Jack's requirements. He understood Samuel's dream was for the farm to be self-sufficient, but Mark's dream would be to build a strong herd and turn the farm into a ranch one day. *With cattle prices low, the opportunity to add to the herd was tempting, but if Samuel was here and he had the money, he'd buy more seed.* Following his conscious this trip, he'd only look at the cattle and ask prices for future reference.

Chapter Sixteen

As Sarah strolled down the wooden walkway, Lydia ran up clutching three long-haired, black and white kittens.

"Ma, can I take one home? Please? The man said I could."

Jack tugged on her dress. "Ma, any news from Grandma and Grandpa? When will Aunt Emma and Uncle Matthew arrive?"

"Wait a minute, Jack, one thing at a time please." Sarah turned to Lydia. She didn't have the heart to say no as Lydia juggled the three fluffy kittens in her arms, with a smile that would have melted her father's heart. "Sweetheart, you can have one kitten. Only one and it will be your responsibility to take good care of it." Lydia's eyes grew wide with delight.

Lydia stretched on her tip toes to kiss her momma on the cheek and said, "Thanks, Ma. I'll take real good care of her."

Nuzzling a kitten in the crook of her right elbow, it was obvious to Sarah which kitten Lydia selected. "Run and tell the man which kitten you want and tell him you'll pick the kitten up tomorrow on our way home."

Lydia rushed back to the stables.

Sarah then turned to Jack. "Yes, Jack, a letter did arrive from back east, but let's wait until tonight before I read it to everyone."

When Lydia returned, all smiles and full of excitement, Sarah said, "Come, Lydia, let's spread the blanket in the church grove for the picnic while Jack goes with Mark to sign up for the Best Shot Competition.

****

Mark and Jack stopped at the hardware store so Jack could take a moment to peek at the guns and knives in the display cabinet.

"I really like the shiny, four-inch blade with a sheath. I could skin any critter with that knife. My knife only has a two and a half inch blade and I can't do much with it," Jack said.

"Not this trip, Jack. Maybe next time." Mark hated the disappointment that dimmed on the boy's face. *I'll talk to Sarah about giving Jack Samuel's knife. It would be something of his father's he could always treasure. I remember putting the knife on the shelf in the tack room the day we buried Samuel.* "Let's go, Jack. We need to get to the sheriff's office so I can sign up for the Competition."

It took Mark only a minute to add his name to the contest entry and pay his five-dollar fee. Walking back to the picnic grove, they overheard three men standing on the wooden walkway discussing politics and what the election of James Buchanan meant to Kansas. Better times ahead Mark hoped. Trips to town were the only chance to catch up on news happening in the rest of the country. Mark paused on purpose behind the men while they talked about other places in Kansas like Atchison, Leavenworth and Topeka which were hit far worse with political unrest than Dead Flats. If things got bad, Mark knew he might have to take the family the two days ride south to Fort Riley. He hoped the pilfering and looting by the ruffians and the fighting and unrest would never bother them, but his gut feeling told him things could get worse before they got better. The issue of slavery always seemed to be a major topic of conversation in town.

Coming from Pennsylvania, Mark favored the free-state cause, not believing in slavery himself, but he refused to discuss politics in public. Samuel had been the same way. Mark smiled as he remembered all their conversations on the topic. The Clark family survived the period known as "Bleeding Kansas" or often called "The Border Wars." Between the years of 1855 and 1858 they managed to stay to themselves during the Border Ruffians attacks, not even venturing to church because of the atrocities and conflict in some areas. Samuel said he wanted no part of state politics that would adversely affect his family.

Mark stopped and bought a copy of the Dead Flat's newspaper, *The Weekly Herald*. He'd read it later and it would give Sarah and the children something new to pour over as well.

They heard a group of men talking about John Brown and the massacre of 1856 that took place along the Missouri and Kansas border two years ago. One man said, 'Now with Abe Lincoln thinking of running for President, the threat of war isn't over and won't be over until slavery is dealt with. There have been different arguments about slavery. One side says government is using the issue to force southern states to join the union. Then others say owning another person isn't right, just because their skin is a different color.' Mark hated the thought of war but realized the possibility. *Thankfully those years are behind us, but slavery is still the cause of fighting.*

Once at the church grove, it didn't take Jack long to spot his momma and Lydia sitting on the blanket. "I'll race you Mark," Jack said, and took off in a dash. Jack won and while Mark caught his breath, Jack asked permission to play ball with a group of boys nearby. Lydia asked if she could go along too.

"Yes, you can both go. Jack, keep an eye on your sister and meet back here in a half hour so we can all watch Mark shoot." The words were barely out of Sarah's mouth and they were gone.

Lydia wore her bonnet and Mark was glad to see her shorn hair wasn't holding her back from joining in and having fun with other children.

Finally, Sarah and Mark were alone with time to themselves. A soft breeze cooled the air as the sun warmed their faces.

Mark settled himself on the blanket. "I have to rest my shooting eye. Will you wake me in time for the shoot?"

"Of course." Sarah rose and carried her shoe-fly pie to the judging table greeting acquaintances along the way. *I don't expect to win the blue ribbon and the two dollar prize money, but it would be nice.* With some free time on her hands, she climbed the stone steps of the Methodist Church.

The pews were empty. A calming silence surrounded her as she sat alone. She had never taken quiet time like this to pray about the past few years. First, losing Richard. Then poor Baby Walter, and just three months later Samuel, the only man she ever loved. She tried to reconcile her sadness with acceptance, but her heart ached with worry and her mind was filled with confusion now that she learned her brother and sister wouldn't be making the trip west as planned.

She sat, trying to put everything into perspective. Looking back over the past months, for the hundredth time, she arrived at the conclusion she wouldn't have made it this far if it hadn't been for Mark. Lydia was alive because of his quick thinking and pocket knife. Sarah tried to count her blessings and, although she was profoundly grateful, she found it difficult to sort out her feelings.

In the serenity of the church, she was startled when she heard a gunshot. *The contest. I must wake Mark.* Jumping to her feet, she ran for the door. When she opened it, to her surprise, Mark and the children were walking toward her. Mark had his arms around the children's shoulders as they headed her way. Smiling faces greeted her and Lydia clapped her hands with excitement. Relief overwhelmed Sarah as she ran to join them. *My, the children have really taken to Mark,* she observed, and acknowledged in her heart for the first time. Of course she was pleased, but she didn't want them to forget about Samuel.

"Come on, Ma, it's time for Mark to shoot. He'll win for sure. He's a great shot," Jack proclaimed as they walked toward Main Street.

Sarah and the children found a good spot in front of the bank to take in the event, saying hello to friends along the way. Mark waited his turn. After ten shooters tried and each missed at least one target, Mark took aim. The first shot hit a paper target one hundred yards away closest to the center. Then three shots shattered three bottles placed at markers along the road at one hundred, one hundred fifty, and two hundred yards. Mark hit them all, then anxiously waited for the last people to shoot. Only one person rivaled Mark's score. The Marshall declared a tie with a shoot-off to determine the winner.

When Mark pulled the trigger on his Sharps to shoot the last bottle at two-hundred yards, the bottle didn't waver. The miss cost him the competition. But the smile on Mark's face told the true story. He was pleased he made it to the shoot-off.

The winner found Mark and asked, "Care to join me for a beer? I'll buy."

"Thanks," Mark said. "Nice offer. Be there in a minute."

****

Making their way through the crowd to congratulate Mark, Sarah overheard the winner say to Mark, "Take your time."

Jack shook Mark's hand and Lydia gave him a hug.

"Well, at least you were close your first try." Sarah smiled. "We'll go to the picnic, and you go celebrate. Come to the blanket when you're finished."

Sarah and the children walked to the church grove, where the women set their dishes of food on the tables. "We may as well go ahead and eat. Mark can eat when he returns," Sarah told the children, and they grabbed plates and headed to take their places in line. There were so many hearty dishes to choose from, not trying a spoonful of everything was a challenge. There was potato salad, cabbage salad, pickled beets and beans, sweet breads, pork, chicken and beef for meat and the list increased with each of the tables. Plates full, the threesome returned to their blanket to enjoy the picnic feast.

After finishing their meals, with a return trip to the food tables for desserts, friends of Jack asked if he wanted to join them in a game of baseball.

"Sure, go ahead, Jack," Sarah told him.

Katy and Hannah Spencer called to Lydia to come to their wagon. Sarah motioned for Lydia to go and she ran to meet them.

Mark still hadn't returned.

Samuel would never have left us alone this long in town with so many strangers about. But just as quickly she reminded herself, *Mark's not Samuel. Oh, how Samuel and I enjoyed our time in town together. We made every minute count. This trip isn't the same without him. But if Mark wants to stay at the saloon all day, that's his business. I hope today doesn't turn into one of the stories he loved to tell the children every time he visited.*

Sarah walked to the dessert table to see if her shoe-fly pie won. *A ribbon would be nice. There's always a chance*, she mused. Looking down at the empty pie plate without a ribbon, she sighed and relaxed her shoulders. Then a smile brightened her spirits. *Someone must have enjoyed my baking.* Her pumpkin pie plates were empty too. She strolled by the food table to see if her pumpkin breads and pickled eggs were gone as well. Everything was cleaned out except for a few pickled eggs. Sarah made small-talk with some of the other women who were gathering their empty dishes.

On her way back to the blanket, Sarah slowed as some townswomen passed her. She wanted to be social. They might think it rude of her not to stop and at least say hello, but there might be questions about the baby, about Samuel, and most certainly, about Mark.

She sighed and approached a group of ladies who stopped talking when they saw her.

"Join us, dear. Sit a spell," Sylvia Turner said in a kind voice.

Sarah sat on the end of the bench. Other ladies greeted her and welcomed her into the conversation as they sat sewing quilt patchwork. Often the church ladies made a quilt to raffle. The money helped defray festival expenses. With any leftover funds, they'd purchase something needed for the church. Sarah had forgotten her fabric this trip and made a mental note to collect some scraps for the next quilt.

"We're glad to see you came to town," one of the ladies said.

"It sure hasn't been an easy year for you after losing your baby and then your husband, my dear," another woman said softly.

"Yes, it's been very difficult," Sarah said in a low voice.

Sylvia Turner raised her head from her sewing long enough to say, "We heard you have a man helping on the farm."

"Yes, we do. We wouldn't have been able to keep the farm if Samuel's best friend, Mark Hewitt, hadn't offered to help. He's been an invaluable help planting the fields. My children have known him all their lives. He's from back home, Pennsylvania."

"Did you get your crops in on time?" Sylvia asked, her head still down.

"Yes, and with Mark's help we were able to clear two additional acres," Sarah shared.

"So he's a work-hand." Sylvia stared, then took a

few more stitches on her quilt patch.

Stiffening a bit at Sylvia's comment, Sarah explained again, "He was a good friend of Samuel's and he doesn't mind helping us. We are grateful for his assistance."

"He's staying to help with the crops, you say?" Sylvia persisted.

"Yes, he said he'd help with the crops and then has to leave for a while," Sarah said sharply.

"Well, my dear, good friend or not, he is a man." Sylvia looked at Sarah and straightened her back.

Infuriated, Sarah stared at Sylvia's near perfect facade, knowing the words were true, but not wanting to acknowledge them. She took a deep breath. "You may mean well, Sylvia, but Mark is a good friend and is helping us as a good friend. That's all. You ladies enjoy your day," she said as she turned, and walked back to the blanket, seething inside.

She sat knees drew to her chest with her arms wrapped around her legs. Sylvia's words with their implied judgement replayed in her mind. Her eyes moistened and she wanted to hide, but the women were looking her way. *They're not going to get the best of me. Not today.* Although she had to admit she was aware her feelings toward Mark were changing. He was no longer only Samuel's friend offering to help with the crops. He was a part of her family's life. *Would Samuel approve?*

Sarah took a few minutes to compose herself and straightened suddenly when Mark dropped to his knees onto the blanket.

"Mark, you startled me," she said, catching her breath.

"Sorry, I didn't mean too."

"That's all right. It wasn't your fault. I was just deep in thought. If you're hungry, you better hurry. Some of the ladies are putting their food away and there's not much left."

Mark dug a plate and fork out of the basket and hurried to the food tables. He returned with a piece of fried chicken in one hand trying to balance a biscuit on top of a spoon full of this and a spoon full that, which covered his entire plate. He sat crossed legged so he could balance his plate in his lap.

Sarah scooted to a corner of the blanket, fearful the ladies were still peering at her and would judge her for sitting too close.

"Perhaps next time," Sarah said, "perhaps next time you'll win the gun. You shot well with very little practice."

"Yes, perhaps next time, if I'm still around." Mark then added quickly to change the subject, "Where are the children?"

"Jack is with his friends and Lydia is with the Spencer girls at their wagon."

As Mark finished eating, Sarah tried to relax. Mark's words, 'If I'm still around' troubled her. *Is he planning on leaving?* She imagined that day might come. A sinking in her gut happened every time Katherine Weaver's name and future plans with Mark came to mind. She didn't want to admit Mark might possibly leave.

Finished at last, Mark said, "The horses need to be fed and I want to check on the wagon. It won't take long. I'll be back soon."

****

A short parade filled the street with onlookers and the four of them joined in the fun. The town band led the way followed by dogs dressed in clothes and performing tricks. A man juggled bottles and another man walked on stilts. Wagons filled with flag waving townspeople followed. They stayed while the politicians spoke, then headed back to the wagon.

Walking back, Martha Spencer's eldest daughter Grace stopped to talk. Mark and Jack continued on to the wagon.

"Would you like to hold the baby?" Grace offered. "She's five months old already."

Baby Walter would have been seven months old in a few days, Sarah's mind took her to the last time she'd held her baby, the day she laid him in Samuel's arms to rest.

Sarah stepped back and said, "No, Grace dear, my hands are dirty. They would soil her beautiful clothes." Then she added, "We're on our way to get cleaned up for the dance. We better hurry along." She took Lydia's hand and walked away.

If my own child isn't alive to hold, another's baby won't do. A piece of me is missing. With Samuel gone, my chances of having another of my own…it's not fair. God, you know how much it meant to me to give Samuel another son. You took away my opportunity. She wanted to run away, to be alone and cry until she was empty of tears. She grabbed her stomach. This incident on top of receiving the news of her father's illness enveloped Sarah. But she understood how much tonight meant to the children, so she shrouded her true feelings, straightened her shoulders, and tried to give an outward appearance of strength.

****

When the music started, the four of them walked to the dance. Fires were burning and tables were piled high with refreshments. The fun just started and immediately Lydia was asked to dance.

Mark spotted Joseph Spencer and made his way to talk. They chatted about the crops, the weather, and the close outcome of the Best Shot Competition. There was a long pause in the conversation before Mark said, "Joseph, you were friends with Samuel. How do you think he would feel if I asked Sarah to marry me?"

"He'd be happy for both of you," Joe answered without hesitating. "He'd rather it was you than anyone else and that's a fact. You were with him when he died. Did he have any last words?"

"He told me to take care of Sarah and his children."

"And that's what you'd be doing," Joe said. "Nobody would think poorly of you. In fact, I'd think poorly of you if you didn't stay. What do you think Sarah would say?"

"I think she'd say yes. At least that's what I want her to say," Mark muttered, shrugging his shoulders.

"Then what are you waiting for?"

"I have another gal waiting for me in Missouri. We discussed getting married someday and I'd want to talk to her first to let her know my plans have changed. Besides, I want to give Sarah plenty of time to grieve. It hasn't been that long."

"You'll know the right time." Joe patted him on the back. "You've never been married before have you, Mark?"

"Nope, this'll be my first."

"Sarah will come around and see marriage is

right."

"Don't say anything to Martha about our talk. I can't ask Sarah yet and want it to keep it quiet until I get things worked out."

"I won't say a word, but don't wait too long. Someone else might get the same idea." Joe pulled some tobacco and paper out of his pocket to roll a smoke and offered them to Mark.

Yeah, someone like Seth Frazer. The idea made Mark cringe.

Before Mark could accept the smoke, Joe's daughter Grace walked up with her baby and handed her to Mark.

"Can you hold Rebecca for me? I'd like to dance this tune," Grace said and rushed out onto the dance floor to join her friends.

The baby girl slept soundly. A little awkward at first, Mark held her to his chest and prayed she wouldn't start crying. He couldn't remember the last time he held a baby.

****

Sarah walked over to talk to Joe's wife, Martha, who gave her a hug. No words were necessary. Martha understood Sarah's situation and wouldn't judge her. A weight lifted from Sarah's shoulders. Martha was a true friend. A feeling of gratitude for the connection rushed warmly through her. They stood and chatted, catching up on the past year.

Then Sarah couldn't hold in her worst fear any longer, "I received word today, my father had a spell with his heart and it will take time for him to recover. My sister and brother aren't coming to stay with us as we planned. They're staying to help care for Father. I certainly understand, but whatever will I do if Mark leaves?"

Martha placed her hand on Sarah's arm and asked, "Have you shared this news with Mark?"

"No, not yet. Mark said he would leave once my brother and sister arrived, but now that they're not coming, I don't know what to do. Mark's other life is waiting for him to return, but my feelings for him are slowly changing into something deeper than gratitude and friendship. I'm beginning to care for him deeply. Martha, is it too soon to have feelings for another man? It's been only four months since Samuel's death."

"My dear, everyone knows how much you loved Samuel. But he isn't here now and you have to think of your children. How will you manage without a man to help with the farm? You can't do it alone. Besides, you've known Mark most of your life. He's a good man."

Sarah's heart finally gave way to her true feelings which were immediately assailed by doubt. "But what if Mark doesn't have the same feelings for me?" *Mark, where is Mark?* And then she spotted him standing beside Joe, holding little Rebecca. The child lay against his chest, sleeping contentedly as Mark gently swayed to the music. He looked so natural holding the child, the same way Samuel looked holding Jack and Lydia. She closed her eyes trying to see a mental picture of Samuel holding their baby, but instead envisioned Mark cradling a baby in his arms. *Mark a father?*

"Well, he's with you at the farm for now," Martha said, following Sarah's gaze to see Mark holding her grandchild. "Maybe there's hope." she offered. "But you must tell him about the news of your father and how it changes your plans."

"I will, but there hasn't been a good time. I didn't want to spoil the day for the children and we don't have much time to talk alone."

****

Mark wanted to dance with Sarah, to feel her in his arms. Nervous she might say no, Mark waited until she swayed to the music and looked out over the crowd for the children. Then he took her hand and swept her into the crowd and stepped to the music without missing a beat. Sarah literally fell into his arms, closed her eyes for a moment and then smiled as they danced effortlessly moving as one. Mark held her tight, closer than socially acceptable. Mark had seen Sarah dance when she was younger. Samuel would ask her to dance every dance. This was Mark's opportunity.

As they glided across the dance floor, heads turned, but Mark didn't care. He knew with certainty he loved Sarah and wanted everyone to notice. Sarah offered no resistance as Mark gazed into her eyes. A serious notion about Katherine hadn't crossed his mind once this evening. His attention was focused on Sarah and the children.

At evening's end, a display of fireworks exploded into colors and streaked across the night sky. The smell of Sulphur lingered and everyone covered their ears when loud explosions rang in the air. The children enjoyed the festivities and that brought a smile to Sarah's face, a smile Mark hadn't seen since before Samuel's death.

Chapter Seventeen

The family awoke before dawn to get an early start on the day. After breakfast, Mark walked to the stables with Lydia to pick up her kitten. Lydia found the little fluff-ball curled up with her mother and picked her up right away. "This one's my favorite," Lydia told Mark, and nuzzled it to her cheek. Looking around Lydia didn't see the other kittens.

Lydia called "Thanks for the kitten" to the nice man in the office, then asked, "Where are the rest of the kittens? There were four of them the other day."

The man called back, "The other kittens have already been taken. Yours is the last one to be picked up. We get stray cats here all the time. It's warm, dry, and there's plenty of mice to hunt so they stay. You can take the mother cat too if you want. I'm sure more will turn up soon."

The mother cat rubbed up against Mark's legs and meowed loudly. Lydia and Mark walked out of the livery and the mother cat followed. They started down the wooden walkway and the mother cat kept in step with them following behind.

Lydia turned around and stopped. The mother cat rubbed against her legs and when Lydia looked up at Mark, he knew her question before she asked. He scooped the mother cat up into his arms and said, "Let me do the talking when we get back to the wagon, but you'll have to take care of them. Are you willing?"

Lydia smiled and shook her head. "Thanks Mark. It's just not right to take the last kitten from her mother."

Arriving at the wagon with both animals, Mark explained the situation to Sarah.

"You softy. You're worse than I am," is all Sarah said, knowing she would have done the same.

As the sun peeked over the horizon, everything was packed and they were ready to set out. Already the heat rippled in waves over the grassy fields, distorting objects in the distance. It would be a scorching ride home, but off in the distance dark rain clouds offered a chance for a little relief.

A few miles down the road, Sarah took the reins from Jack and he crawled over the seat to play with Lydia and the cats. When Sarah looked back a few minutes later, the kitten was sound asleep in Lydia's arms and the mother cat was curled up on Jack lap. Jack and Lydia's eyelids were drooping, too. With the warmth of the morning sun and the wagon's gentle rock, soon her children were also asleep.

This was the opportunity Sarah had waited for. She motioned for Mark to come sit beside her. He tied Ruby to the wagon, climbed up on the seat and took the reins.

Whispering, so not to wake the children, Sarah said, "My father had a spell with his heart, and it will take time for him to recover. This means my sister and brother won't be coming this year. They can't leave Mother alone by herself to care for Father. I sent a letter to console Mother and explained, I understood the family's decision. My parents have always been there for us. I knew one of them taking ill was always a possibility, but I didn't know my father had a heart condition. I so wish I could be there." Sarah brushed away an escaping tear.

Mark placed his arm around her shoulders. Comforted by his embrace, she was silent for a few moments. Then, struggling to hold back more tears, she said, "Mark, you have done so much already, especially when you paid off the general store bill. The owner told me my bill was paid-in-full. You helped us clear land, bought us seed and supplies, and helped us with the crops and the cattle. And I'll never be able to thank you enough for saving my daughter's life." Tears spilled down Sarah's cheeks. "I hate to think of the outcome if you weren't there."

Mark remained silent, but Sarah sensed his understanding and his support because each time she mentioned his good deeds, he gave a gentle squeeze to her shoulder.

After a long pause, Sarah said, "Perhaps we should return east to take care of my parents and be with my family. Now that things have changed my mind is spinning, not knowing what to do when you have to leave us." This was as close to admitting her feelings for Mark as Sarah dared to mention.

****

They sat in silence for a while. Then Mark said, "Sarah the farm meant everything to Samuel. He was so proud of you and his children and all you built together. He often told me his plans. He wanted to give you and the children a good life. He was always thinking and planning ahead.

"Why don't you take some time to really think things over? There's no need to make a hasty decision.

My promise to Samuel, my word given to him still stands. He asked me to look out for you and the children and that's exactly my plan unless you kick me out." He chuckled. "Whatever you decide, it's your decision, Sarah. But please weigh all the options first."

Sarah leaned against Mark's comforting arm while they traveled the well-used, dusty path in silence until the children awoke.

"Come on, everyone, out of the wagon." Sarah stretched and yawned. "We can all use a break."

Everyone enjoyed watching the fluffy black and white kitten Lydia named Muzzy, pounce and play in the tall grass with her mother, Momma Kitty, before continuing on their way, refreshed.

Sarah tried to make the time pass as she talked about everything that happened in town. She started with the parade, then their friends, the dance and ended with the evening fireworks. There were some new stores since their last trip. Jack, of course, described the knife at the hardware store in detail and Lydia thanked her momma again for letting her give the kitten and her mother a good home.

The heat and dryness of the day made for miserable traveling. By mid-afternoon, they all agreed another break was much needed. "There's a cluster of trees up ahead. Let's pull into the shade and have a bite to eat." Sarah took the reins from Jack and guided the horses to the shady spot. The rain so hoped for in the morning hadn't arrived and there was no relief in sight.

While Sarah laid out a mid-day meal on the blanket under the shaded of the tall trees, Jack fetched water from the barrel for the horses and Lydia gave some to the cats."

Later in the day, Sarah mentioned, "Maybe we'll spy some game along the way for supper tonight. And if we don't Jack, you and Uncle Mark can go hunting when we stop for the night and see what you can find. We left so early this morning we have a good start on getting home by mid-afternoon tomorrow."

Shadows grew longer until Mark finally announced, "It's time to stop and make camp."

Jack pulled the wagon off the path near some sumac trees, jumped down off the hard, wooden seat, and gathered wood to ready a fire. He then asked, "Do you need anything else, Ma?"

"No, thank you, son. See if you and Uncle Mark can find some small game. No matter what you happen across, the stew will taste better with meat."

"Which way, Uncle Mark?" Jack asked, sitting behind him on Ruby.

"Well, we passed a gully a quarter mile back. There's bound to be something's living there."

While Mark and Jack were hunting, Sarah prepared the stew vegetables and then she and Lydia picked raspberries they found growing wild in the field.

****

At the gully, Mark and Jack dismounted and settled down and waited in silence. Then they heard some rustling in the brush and a grouse stepped out.

Mark motioned to Jack to stay quiet as he leaned forward to get a better shot. When he slowly raised the rifle to his shoulder, the bird flew away.

"Sometimes they get away." Mark shrugged his shoulders. Then the subtle movement of a rabbit twitching its ear was all the motion it took and he shot.

"What was it? Did you get it, Uncle Mark?" Jack

shouted out excitedly.

"A rabbit. Sorry, Jack, there wasn't time to give you notice to cover your ears. Let's go see." Mark let Jack lead the way.

"It's not moving," Jack said.

"Let's make sure first. Nudge it with a stick and if it doesn't breathe, you can pick it up."

Jack did as Mark asked. "You got it," Jack called out, then picked it up by the hind legs and held it high in the air to show it off.

"You don't always return with meat when you go hunting, Jack. We were lucky tonight. Come on. Let's get back." Mark helped Jack up behind him in the saddle and wasted no time heading toward their campsite.

"Your father would be proud of you, Jack. Surely he's smiling right now."

"If only I could tell him how much he's missed. Lydia and I don't say much around Ma, but we think of him every day. Ma misses him too. She cries at night sometimes, but not as often now."

"Anytime you want to talk about your father, you can always talk to me, Jack. Your father was my best friend. We went to school together. You remind me of him in so many ways. You have his smile and his kind eyes. You're level headed, good with the horses, not afraid of a hard day's work, and you love to fish. He'd be very proud of you."

"Thanks, Uncle Mark. It's nice to have someone to talk to," Jack admitted.

Just ahead Mark could see smoke and flickering flames from the camp fire. He held a gaze on Sarah as he and Jack rode in.

"Any luck?" Sarah called to them.

"Uncle Mark shot a rabbit and now he's going to show me how to skin it," Jack blurted out. Your stew will taste swell tonight, Ma. And we can give some of the meat to the cats."

Later in the evening, sitting around the campfire, Jack told the hunting story. The excitement in his voice as he recalled the hunt touched Mark deeply.

"All right, it's time for bed," Mark announced.

"What about Grandma's letter, Ma? You never read it to us," Jack said.

"Sorry. You're right, Jack. Let's keep the letter until we get home and can sit around the table and enjoy Grandma's words together."

The children fussed a little, but then Lydia gently lifted Muzzy and Momma Kitty into the wagon to sleep with her while Jack cuddled in his quilt under the wagon. Sarah and Mark wished them sweet dreams and joined one another for a last cup of tea.

****

The next morning, Mark awoke before daybreak. *The air is cool now, but the sky is clear. It looks like the making of another miserably hot day. Hope we can make it home before it gets too bad.* He added wood to last night's fire so Sarah could make a pot of tea and breakfast.

Mark estimated they were only three hours from home. Thinking of home, he wondered how Seth Frazer made out with the chores, if he picked up the seed, and if he finished the whole cake himself. By the time Mark fed the horses, the rest of the family was up and ready for the day.

Sarah serve breakfast and Mark assisted. The smell

of potatoes and onions along with Mark's contribution of freshly made wood ash biscuits filled the air. Mark sat on the ground to eat and his eyes gravitated toward Sarah again and followed her every movement. He took in every detail like the curve of her back when she leaned over the fire to pour tea and the graceful way she sat beside her daughter with her skirt tucked neatly under her legs to guard off bugs. It didn't matter what she did, he couldn't take his eyes off her. Then she glanced his way, and Mark thought for sure she could read his mind. He wanted to tell her he loved her, but how? He couldn't just blurt it out. The timing had to be right.

****

Playing with the cats helped pass the time for Lydia and Jack even though the bright sun and heat made the ride very uncomfortable. They finally arrived at the farm about noon. As the cats explored their new surroundings, Lydia made a bed for them in the barn. Mark and Jack unhitched the horses, rubbed them down and did chores, while Sarah fixed a mid-day meal.

"After we eat, I'll read Grandma's letter," Sarah told the children, dishing-up fresh greens from the garden and fried vegetables from the root cellar. It wasn't much, but it sure tasted good. Sarah made a cobbler with the raspberries she and Lydia picked and it smelled fragrant while it cooked in the oven.

After the meal and the dishes were done, the children sat, one on each side of their momma, at the kitchen table while Sarah read aloud. The letter told of their grandpa's heart condition, the fact that their aunt and uncle would be staying in Pennsylvania to take care of him and that their family back east loved and missed them. When she finished, the children were saddened by the news of their grandpa and hugged their momma.

Jack recalled his memories of his grandfather. "He always fixed us bacon for breakfast, rocked on the front porch, played cards and checkers with us, and smoked a pipe after supper."

Lydia added, "And he always planted a big garden."

Sarah couldn't hold her emotions and her eyes welled with tears.

"Grandpa's illness was unexpected. Aunt Emma and Uncle Matthew have to stay and help Grandma now. It's disappointing, but Grandma needs them and of course they needed to be there. You can understand, right?"

Jack and Lydia nodded, tears spilled onto Lydia's cheeks and Jack struggled to keep his composure.

"Without your aunt and uncle's help, this year's harvest won't be easy," Sarah said. "It will mean long days and hard work, possibly the hardest work you've ever done."

Jack looked at Lydia and then at their momma. "We understand, Ma. Lydia and I talked about this after Poppa died. We thought you might want to go back east then. But what would we do if we did go back? We wouldn't own anything and could only take with us what we could carry in the wagon. We know the harvest will be hard work, but we've made it this far and we don't want to give up on Poppa's dream. It's our dream now, too."

Jack said exactly what Sarah needed to hear. Jack was right and she didn't have an answer to his question. She had asked herself the same thing...what would they do if they did go back east?

Jack stood beside his momma and asked, "Isn't this the farm you and Poppa always dreamed of? Isn't living here the reason we left our friends and family in Pennsylvania and joined the wagon train in the first place? Poppa died providing for us, Ma. We owe it to him not to lose what you both worked so hard to build. Farming is hard work, but we love it here. This is our home and we want to stay."

Lydia gave her momma a big hug that said it all.

Sarah had made up her mind. How the children took the news would determine their fate. With an arm around each child, holding them close, she looked at Mark, knowing it would be impossible to run the farm without him.

"I'll stay to see you through the harvest," Mark said. "When winter comes, I'll have to leave for a few months to set a trap line for some extra money. But I'll come back in the spring and help you clear a few more acres and plant the crops."

Hearing Mark's words, Sarah had her answer.

Lydia looked at her momma and asked, "Why are you crying, Ma?"

"These are happy tears, sweetheart. We're making the right decision. We aren't going anywhere. Knowing you children want to stay and grow up here means so much to me. I'm sure your father is smiling down on us all right now." Sarah sniffled, blinked away some tears and tried to smile.

"I've never cried happy tears," Lydia said.

"You will someday," Sarah assured her. "You will someday."

Later, as Sarah tucked Lydia into bed, Lydia said,

"Can we take more milk to the barn as soon as morning comes? Muzzy and Momma Kitty will be hungry. Do you think they're sleeping in the crate I fixed them?"

"Yes, dear. We can take the cats some milk in the morning. Muzzy is sleeping just fine, wherever she is in the barn. They may even cuddle up beside Mark tonight. Now get some sleep. You'll see them in the morning."

After Mark left for the barn, Sarah took a lantern, walked up the hill to Samuel's grave, and sat on the ground beside the cross.

"I miss you so much, Samuel. I still don't see why God took you from us when we truly need you here. The children miss you terribly. Mark being here has helped them through some rough times and, if I'm completely honest, he's helped me, too.

"The fields are planted and so far it's been a good year with ample rain. Our harvest should be a good one so we can pay off our debt at the hardware. Mark already paid off the general store for us with some money from his gold claim. But you already know all of this, as I'm sure you are watching out for us from above.

"Samuel, I need to tell you about a change in my feelings for Mark. He was your good friend and he has been nothing but a gentleman to me. He is a trusted ally and was a much appreciated shoulder to cry on when I needed support after learning Matthew and Emma couldn't come because of Father's heart condition.

"I'm sure you heard the children say they want to stay here in Kansas and make this their home. When they asked what we would do if we returned east, I didn't have an answer for them. I really don't want to give up our farm either. When Mark said he would stay to help and come back in the spring, my heart filled with gratitude. Suddenly, because of his assurance, I know everything will work out. Because of Mark, we will be able to stay here on the farm.

"What I've been putting off telling you, Samuel, is that I'm beginning to have deeper feeling for Mark. Samuel, you will always be my first true love. Please know, this comes from the bottom of my heart. I will always love you. But I have to think about the children and the rest of my life. Mark is teaching Jack how to hunt and work the fields and he loves Jack and Lydia very much. He'll always have my gratitude. He saved Lydia's life.

"All right, I'm just going to say it, Samuel. I'm developing feeling for Mark. I didn't plan for this to happen. I didn't realize they were true feelings until this trip to town. Please don't be upset, I don't even know if Mark has true feeling for me, but I believe he does. What should I do Samuel? I pray you'll understand. If only I knew." Sarah gazed up into the starry night and brushed away a tear. Then, just as she was about to look away, a light streaked across the sky. Then another, and yet another falling star streamed toward earth. She took this as a sign from Samuel. He understood. Her heart warmed thinking about Samuel's way of showing his approval.

But what about Mark and Katherine Weaver. Mark had told Samuel he loved Katherine and planned to marry her. Sarah's chest constricted at the thought that Katherine Weaver really had claim on Mark and her own feelings would have to take second position. She knew Mark would have to see Katherine and it frightened her. *What if she persuades him to stay with her?* Sarah's mind whirled with anxiety.

Walking back to the house, Sarah glanced at the barn and there was lamp light coming from within. Mark had gone to the barn hours ago. Why was he still awake? She called to him and he invited her to join him. They sat in the barn on the back of the spring wagon and started reminiscing about old times and remembering some of the jokes Samuel used to play on them. "Two of his favorites," Sarah recalled, "were using tomatoes to fake blood and pretending to break his arm to get out of chopping wood."

Sarah finally relaxed as Mark shared again Samuel's final words, "Tell Sarah I love her." And he repeated his own promise to Samuel, "I'll take care of your family for you. Don't worry, they will be safe." Hearing these words spoken by Mark again filled her soul with hope and joy.

Although exhausted from the day's activities, they talked late into the night. They both needed this time to share as friends and grieve for Samuel who was so special to them both.

As Sarah walked to the house, she was at a new place with Samuel's passing. At last she rested easy knowing Samuel understood her feeling for Mark. At least Mark would be with them through the harvest. She and the children could keep Samuel's dream alive. She'd take it a day at a time, keeping close to herself the new feelings she had toward Mark.

Chapter Eighteen

Warm, sunny days with ample rain turned the fields into blankets of green and produced vegetables on the vines in the garden.

One night Sarah served a stew made with beef, diced potatoes, and carrots for color and topped with rolled, square-cut noodles in the Pennsylvania style. "What a meal," Mark said, as he took a piece of freshly baked bread and mopped his plate, not leaving so much as a drop of broth. The children enthusiastically mimicked his actions.

"There's more if you'd like, Mark. Another plateful maybe?" Sarah offered.

"No thanks. I'm saving room for a piece of your pie with a cup of coffee later."

Pie and coffee made Mark think of Seth Frazer, whose supplies were still in the barn. It had been more than a week since they returned from town. Seth had taken the vegetable seeds and the six seed potatoes Mark left for him. Seth also left an empty cake pan and an empty kettle, both scrubbed clean.

While the children were doing dishes before dessert could be served, Mark told one of his famous cowhand stories. By the time he finished, Jack and Lydia were laughing so hard they were almost crying and Sarah was smiling from ear to ear. Then Mark reminded everyone, "We all need a goodnight's sleep because tomorrow we're tackling the corral. Your father would be very proud of his herd and even prouder of his family. You children and your mother have worked hard."

After tucking in the children and saying prayers, Sarah prepared two plates of pie.

Mark, seeing the knife in Sarah's hand, remembered his idea of giving Jack his Pa's knife and said, "Sarah, watching Jack at the hardware store day dreaming about one day owning his own knife made me think of Samuel's knife. It's in the barn on the top shelf. It wouldn't be new, but it would be his father's. He's old enough to take care of it and treat it with respect. In the morning you can decide if you want to give it to him now or wait."

"Giving Jack his father's knife is a great idea, Mark. Jack's responsible enough to use it properly," Sarah said, and joined Mark at the table where the two of them sat and talked while they enjoyed their pie and coffee in the quiet of the evening.

"The meal you served tonight sure was delicious, Sarah. It brought back memories of my mother and the smells of her kitchen. Thank you." Mark slid his hand across the table and gently cupped Sarah's hand in his.

Sarah beamed. "Oh, you're welcome Mark. Glad you enjoyed it."

"And thank you again for the pie and coffee." Mark stood. "Off to bed. We both need to get a good night's sleep." Walking out the door, he turned back for one more look at Sarah, then said, "Goodnight."

****

Noises she heard coming from the kitchen awoke Sarah the next morning. *It's Samuel and he's sure to be hungry,* she sprang to her feet. Thinking she must have overslept, she dressed quickly and rushed through the kitchen, grabbing the bucket to fetch water, but stopped cold when she looked out the door and saw Mark chopping wood. *Mark was making the noise, not Samuel. Of course, it couldn't have been Samuel.*

Mark is the man who's been taking care of us. He's the man who has come to know and share the same love for the children and the farm as Samuel. A calm warmth overwhelmed her heart. *My trust in Mark has grown these past few months. He has become the man of this house, the man who protects us and cares for us. He saved Lydia's life and taught Jack about working the fields and hunting.* Sarah took a deep breath and let it out slowly. *My love for Mark is true love. Oh, Samuel, you showed me last night with the shooting stars that you approved.*

Sarah sighed. Samuel's presence and love filled her again with peace instead of the conflict that had swirled in her mind since his death. Yes, Samuel gave her his blessing.

Again she reminded herself, *Mark's heart is already taken. Is it wrong of me to fall in love with a man whose heart is already promised to another? What about Miss Katherine Weaver? Does Mark still love her? Will he leave us and go back to be with her? He said he'd stay until the crops are harvested, but can he wait that long to see her again?*

Sarah stood, distracted, bucket in hand, when she heard Mark called out, "Good morning. Do you need a hand with the water, Sarah?"

Sarah waved and called, "No, it's not heavy. The coffee will be ready soon. Come in when you finish."

"Sounds good. What's for breakfast?"

"How about flapjacks with maple syrup?"

"Sounds great with a cup of coffee. Be right in."

Sarah filled her pail and walked back inside glancing at the old clock on the wall as she passed. She wasn't late. The time was right, exactly the right time for everything. She didn't know if Mark had the same feelings for her. She would have to wait until time brought her the answers.

Entering the house, Mark handed Sarah Samuel's knife which she placed in the cupboard. After breakfast, Mark offered to show Jack how to set a snare to catch the rabbit spotted in the garden.

Sarah winked at Mark. When Jack caught the rabbit, she'd give him his father's knife.

****

The next afternoon while Sarah weeded the garden, Seth Frazer approached in his wagon. Sarah stepped out of the garden, wiped her hands on her apron and fixed her hair before she greeted him. "Hello, Seth. Please, get down and join me for a glass of cool tea. Are you thirsty?

"Thank you, Sarah, but no tea right now."

"It's good to see you, Seth. It's been awhile. Thank you for coming on such short notice to take care of the livestock. I trust the cake met with your approval," she said with a big smile.

"Your cooking was never hard to eat, Sarah. Why, even on the wagon trail your camp always had the best food."

"Did you come to pick up your supplies?"

"Yes, but that's not the only reason, Sarah. The other is to pay my respects to you. Samuel was a good man and he helped me get through Anne's death. How are you doing, Sarah?"

"Oh, I'm doing all right. You met Mark the other week. He's been my rock these last few months. He helped with the planting. Did you see the back fields on your ride in? You can see they're doing well and so is my vegetable garden." She extended her arm, sweeping the length of the garden. "We'll have a full harvest this year, if the weather cooperates."

"That's great, and thanks for the seed and the potatoes. My garden is doing well too. Glad things are going well for you, Sarah. Mark mentioned you were hoping for a letter from home. Did it arrive?"

"Yes. Thank you for asking, it contained sad news. My father had a spell with his heart and now my brother and sister won't be coming west as first planned. They're going to stay and help Mother take care of him."

"Sorry to hear about your father. I'm sure you're disappointed about your family not coming. May I ask, what your plans are now?"

"We are staying right here," Sarah said with confidence. "The children don't want to go back east and, with Mark's help, we will be fine. He's going to stay until November, then set a trap line for some extra income over the winter and come back next spring to check on us. As you see, Jack's growing like a weed and he can handle the chores while Mark's away."

They were quiet for a moment, then Seth asked, "Could we go to Samuel's grave to pay my respects?"

"Of course, we can walk to the old elm tree. Samuel and our baby are buried there together. We named our child Walter Samuel Clark. When Samuel died, we buried Samuel with the baby in his arms. Now they rest together next to Brother Richard under the old elm tree."

"So sorry for your losses. You've had a year of sadness weighing on your heart. Is there anything you need help with? Jack knows the way to my place. If there's anything you ever need, send him right away. Please, Sarah," Seth said, as he took her hand and looked into her eyes.

Seth was a good friend. Sarah knew he meant what he said. Tears fell and she quickly brushed them away. "No, really, we are fine."

"It takes time. Give it some time, Sarah. It will get easier." Seth wiped a tear from her cheek with his thumb. "At least it has for me. You'll always grieve for Samuel. Not a day goes by that..." His voice trailed off.

"Yes, Samuel is missed terribly, but he's with God now." Sarah brushed her cheek again. "His death was an accident. Nobody was to blame. Anne's death was an accident too. You shouldn't still blame yourself, Seth. Nobody blames you. Anne wouldn't hold you accountable for her accident. And that's what it was, an unfortunate accident, just like Samuel's death.

"We have to deal with our losses. My husband is gone and it's not the same. It will never be the same, but life continues. We have to make a new life now and look to the future.

"Anne was my friend and so were the Millers who got sick along the trail. We must have been crazy to leave our family and friends in Pennsylvania, but we did it and nobody could talk us out of it. We were young, fearless, and brave. We could do anything and we did, and now here we are."

"It didn't work out quite the way we planned, did it Sarah?" Seth looked down.

Sarah looked down too, shook her head, and let Seth continue.

"You're right, Sarah, we have to go on, look toward the future. Anne wouldn't want me to give up. My life hasn't been the same these past four years, barely existing, and all alone.

"Samuel tried to tell me the same thing you just told me. Samuel wouldn't want you to blame yourself either, Sarah. You have to be strong for your children. You need each other.

"I need to make changes in my life too. Changes for the better."

Sarah gave Seth a friendly hug. "Good, Seth. Anne would be so happy you're moving forward with your life. It is possible to love again, and it looks like you've taken the first step to open your heart."

Chapter Nineteen

Mark observed the exchange between Sarah and Seth from the house. Sudden concern made his throat tighten. He admitted he didn't like seeing Seth paying affectionate attention to Sarah. Seth looked nothing like the disheveled man Mark recalled first meeting. Now he was clean-shaven and in presentable clothes.

A question formed in Mark's mind, *Could Sarah and Seth have feelings for each other?* Suddenly it seemed like a good time to give Seth a hand with the supplies. Mark ran his fingers through his hair, stepped out the door and called, "Hello, Seth. We wondered when you'd arrive. Thanks again for taking care of the animals so we could go to town. The trip was long, but a good one. We picked up those supplies you wanted."

Sarah spoke slowly, "Yes, the children were tired from the journey and I had yet to tell them about their grandfather's illness and that their aunt and uncle wouldn't be coming to live with us."

Hearing the tension in Sarah's voice, Mark made a bold gesture and gently placed his hand on Sarah's shoulder to comfort her. "Come with me, Seth, your supplies are in the barn. I'll help you load up so you can get going. Sarah, why don't you find the children? They'll want to say hello to Seth before he has to leave."

Seth turned toward Sarah, "Would it be possible to

beg a meal and a place to bunk for the night? It's time for me to continue my life. I plan to head to town tomorrow."

Sarah gave Seth a hug. "You're always welcome here, Seth Frazer. Of course you can stay. Anytime. The children will be glad to see you."

Seth extended his bent arm to Sarah, a gentlemanly gesture, she took it and they walked to the house.

Mark combed back his hair with his fingers, put his hands in his pockets, and hung his head. He called to Sarah, "The children are out behind the barn. We'll be in soon." Not wanting to leave them alone for too long, he quickly found the children playing with Muzzy and Momma Kitty. Waving to get their attention, he called, "Your momma would like you to come say hello to Mr. Frazer."

Walking into the house, he didn't want to appear over protective or jealous, but that was exactly what he was...jealous.

****

After dinner, they sat around the table reminiscing about the long wagon train ride west. Mr. Frazer recalled stories for the children.

"Remember all the fights stirred up amongst the families? I wondered at times if we'd ever arrive in Kansas," Seth began. He then started right into a story the children would remember about a bear. "It was the largest bear spotted on the whole trip and it cozied up to the chuck wagon and almost tore off the canvas," Seth recalled.

Finally, he told his last story. "On the way here today, a long, ring-neck snake surprised me. I was in the creek filling the water barrel and it lay by a log watching my every move."

Story telling over, Sarah hurried the children to bed.

Uneasy with Mark while Sarah tended the children, Seth began, "The fields look good this year, Mark, and thanks for the extra seed you left for me. It's all planted."

Mark countered with, "Getting two additional acres planted took work. Even Sarah and Lydia helped in the fields doing what they could." Then Mark lowered his voice, "Did Sarah mention her father's illness and her brother and sister aren't coming this fall?"

"Yes, she told me."

"When Samuel died, he made me promise to take care of his family and it is my intention to keep my promise," Mark said, again in a low voice. As Sarah climbed down the ladder from the loft, Mark stood and stretched, "Well, if you want to get an early start for town in the morning, we better turn in and get some sleep, Seth."

Sarah handed Seth a towel, pillow, and blanket.

"There should be plenty of water in the pitcher on the porch to wash, Seth," she said.

"You can bunk in the barn with me," Mark offered, before Sarah could offer a spot in the house.

Seth accepted the offer to sleep in the barn and then stepped out onto the porch.

"Do you need anything done yet tonight, Sarah?" Mark offered.

"No, nothing. Thank you, Mark."

"Okay," Mark said turning at the door to take one last look at Sarah. This became part of his nightly routine, a final glimpse for the day of the woman he'd developed special feelings for. No, the woman he loved.

Seth fashioned a bed out of hay and settled down for the night.

Mark lay awake a long time thinking of the exchange he witnessed earlier between Sarah and Seth. He'd have to remember to extend his arm to Sarah sometime.

The following morning, Sarah cooked breakfast while Seth helped Mark and Jack with the barn chores. After eating, Seth was ready to head for Dead Flats.

"No reason to haul those supplies to town and back." Seth jumped into the wagon and picked up the reins.

"All right then. We'll see you on your way back through." Sarah handed Seth a basket of food.

"It might be a few weeks. My animals at home will be fine. They have access to the creek for water and the pasture is rich with grasses. I let the milk cow dry up weeks ago," Seth said.

"Well, we'll see you whenever you return. And plan on supper and spending the night," Sarah added.

"Be careful and don't get into any trouble," Jack called after him.

Mark stood deliberately close to Sarah as Seth rode out so it looked like his arm was around her waist which is exactly what Mark wanted Seth to think. He didn't want Seth Frazer getting too cozy with Sarah. He waved glad to see Seth leaving for Dead Flats on a warm morning with what appeared to be rain clouds in the distance. The crops could use a good shower.

****

Jack ran, anxious to check his snare. As he rounded

the corner of the house, sure enough there was a rabbit caught in the trap. He couldn't wait to tell Mark.

"Grab a long piece of firewood from the pile, Jack," Mark called to him.

Without hesitation, Jack poked the rabbit to make sure it wasn't breathing before he removed it from the snare and proudly carried it to show to his momma and Lydia.

"Can I use your knife to skin it, Mark?"

"No need. Wait right here, Jack." Sarah rushed into the house to fetch Samuel's hunting knife, returned, and handed it to Jack.

"This is Pa's knife!"

"Yes, and now it's yours, son. I know you're responsible and will take care of it. Your pa would want you to have it."

"Mine to use and keep sharp, like Pa?"

Sarah beamed with delight.

Jack slid the knife from the sheath, tested the sharpness with his thumb as he'd seen his poppa do so many times, and lifted his head smiling. "Can we have rabbit stew for supper tonight?"

"Of course." Sarah hugged Jack. "Your father would be very proud of you."

Chapter Twenty

Mark and Sarah would often take walks together to enjoy the evening air and talk about the day's activities on the farm. Mark became aware of how her hair made a perfect little curl at the nape of her neck. Once, as he helped her over a fallen log, her small hand slipped into his. Yes, it was calloused from hard work, but was the most precious hand he ever held and he was careful to be gentle. Walking the path back from the fields after a rain, he slipped his arm around Sarah's waist to scoop her up in his arms and carry her over a water puddle stretching across the road. He marveled at her slimness and warmth.

Staying up to talk, playing cards and checkers, losing track of time when they were together became a habit. They were able to talk about Samuel and share stories about him with each other. Sarah even smiled and laughed more often.

Mark had developed a true heart-connection with Sarah but wasn't sure how to express his feelings so they wouldn't be misunderstood. Then, one night, he awoke from a dream in which he cradled a baby in his arms. The baby slept relaxed and contented. In the dream, he looked across the room and a woman stood at a stove. She wore a ring on her finger. She turned and looked at him. Katherine Weaver!

Awake and confused, it took Mark a moment to

orient himself. He lay wondering, *do I really love Katherine? Was this dream to remind me of the future we could share? But Sarah needs me. Am I staying here on the farm only because Samuel asked me to take care of Sarah, or was I truly in love with her? If I weren't here, would she find someone else? Maybe, Seth Frazer?* As Mark remembered Seth's caring tone of voice when talking about Sarah, jealousy overcame him. He tossed and turned the rest of the night, asking himself questions he wasn't able to answer. As the light of dawn crept into the barn, he realized it didn't matter if he loved Sarah if she didn't feel the same about him. He needed to know her feelings.

The next day, after the children hurried to do their chores, Mark sat drinking his second cup of coffee while gazing at Sarah in the kitchen. It took a moment before it registered she'd said something to him. His mind was on last night's dream.

"What are your plans for today, Mark?" Sarah asked.

"I thought I'd ride out and check on the back fields. Would you like to ride along?"

"It's been awhile since I've ridden."

"Well, don't let that stop you. It's not far. Some fresh air would be good for both of us. In fact, let's make it a picnic."

"All right," Sarah said, without hesitation. She gathered a hasty mid-day meal and gave instructions to the children. "Jack and Lydia, the two of you are old enough to be alone for a few hours while Mark and I take a ride. Ring the dinner bell if anything happens and you need help. We won't go far."

"You can count on me, Momma," Jack said.

"Lydia and I will be fine."

Mark cupped his hands to boost Sarah onto Button and they rode off.

Riding past the lush green crops, Mark began, "Samuel asked me to help you and the children. If we hadn't planted the crops you might have lost your farm."

"Is the only reason you're still here because Samuel asked you to help us?" Sarah asked with hesitation, reluctant to mention the subject of when Mark would leave.

"Well, it's one of the reasons why we're taking this ride today. Let's cross the creek and spread the quilt so we can sit and talk."

Mark spread the quilt in silence watching Sarah's every move. He sat on one corner across from her, then couldn't wait any longer. He had to know. Leaning forward, he shared, "Over these past few months, my feelings for you have grown, Sarah. We've gotten to know each other better and your children are very special. Is there any chance you have some feelings for me? I mean…" Mark's throat tightened and his heart pounded. He took a deep breath, then looked into her eyes and continued, "I couldn't help notice you and Seth Frazer walked together arm-in-arm. Do you have feelings for him?"

"Stop, Mark." Clasping his hands in hers, Sarah looked him directly in the eyes and said, "No, there are no feelings for Seth. My feelings run deep for you. They weren't always there, and then they just happened. My first indication occurred in town over the Fourth of July. When you swept me in your arms to dance, you melted away all my fears. I hadn't told you about my father's illness yet, and I didn't know your plans, but you made something stir in my heart."

"Really?" Mark broke a grin. He inched closer across the blanket, close enough to be aware of her breath. "My intentions weren't to fall in love with you, Sarah. We want the same things in life. My love for Jack and Lydia are as if they are my own. But you were always Samuel's girl. I took a chance at the dance. I just wanted to hold you in my arms and feel you close to me. If you had pulled back, I wouldn't have pursued my efforts. But you didn't."

"Honestly, Mark, my feelings are the same for you. It has only been a short time since Samuel's death and I mean no disrespect. I think he would approve. We didn't set out to have this connection."

Sarah's demeanor quickly changed as she asked, "But what about Katherine? Samuel couldn't wait to tell me you found a girl you hoped to marry. Knowing she was a part of your life made me worry you would leave us and return to her."

Understanding lit Mark's face as he put all the pieces of the puzzle into place. "So Samuel couldn't keep my secret. He said he wouldn't tell you about Katherine. You were to be surprised when the announcement was made, but of course, he couldn't wait. Naturally you would wonder about my intentions."

Now, Sarah had to know. "Have you seen Katherine since Samuel's death?"

"No, Sarah. Christmas was the last time we were together, but I sent a letter explaining the situation, my promise to Samuel, and that my commitment here wouldn't be over until after the harvest. Now I'll need to tell Katherine in person our relationship is over." Mark took a deep breath and sighed. "You say you have feelings for me, Sarah. Is it too soon for you to feel love?"

"Yes. No. Yes," Sarah said, blushing in joy and confusion, "I do love you, Mark."

Mark cupped Sarah's face in his hands anticipating her sweet taste as his warm lips brushed hers. Pulling back suddenly, he said wide-eyed, "What about the children? What will they think about me staying on permanent and loving their mother? Samuel will always be their father, but do you think they will accept me?"

Smiling, Sarah said, "Jack may have wanted to be the man of the family after his father died, but he soon discovered if you hadn't stayed, we were in jeopardy of losing the farm. You heard Jack and Lydia say this farm means everything to them, and it means a lot to you too. The children love you, Mark. They have always loved you. They won't have a problem accepting you into our family. But let's not say anything to them for a little while. Let's take some time and make sure this is what we both want."

"Okay, we'll keep our feelings from the children for now, but it won't be easy. I love you so much, Sarah." Mark gently encircled her with his strong arms as he kissed her tenderly.

Sarah's heart fluttered. A rush of warmth started in her belly and rose up her body enfolding her heart to bloom on her cheeks. Being this close to Mark in this intimate manner filled her with anticipation and hope. She had dared to envision this moment and it was everything she dreamed it would be and more. Mark truly cared for her and the children and now someday could be her husband.

Mark rested his forehead against hers, "We won't rush into anything, Sarah."

They laid on the quilt in silence with Sarah snug against Mark's side as they both gazed up at the light blue Kansas sky. Sarah said she loved him. This was the answer he longed to hear. This changed everything. His world would be complete with a wife and a family to love. He needed to speak with Katherine as soon as possible.

As he lay dreaming of his future with Sarah, he wondered if she would consider another child...his child. This wasn't the right time to discuss the topic, it could wait for Sarah to decide later after all the pain and heartache she experienced lessened a little.

After what seemed like minutes, but was really much longer, Sarah said, "We'd better head home. The children might start worrying."

"Okay," Mark agreed. "But what about our picnic?"

"Next time we have a picnic we should leave time to eat the food." Sarah laughed. "Please say we can do this again soon, Mark."

"Of course we can. How about tomorrow?" Mark grinned.

****

Back at the house, Jack wanted to surprise his mother and sweep the floor. As he worked the broom around his mother's rocking chair, he accidently bumped the side table and the picture of James and Mary Miller's house fell to the floor. Hoping Lydia hadn't heard the fall, Jack inspected the treasure. The corner of the frame was cracked and barely attached.

Nothing a little pitch from the red cedar wouldn't fix. Carefully he returned the picture to the table. He'd remember to get some pitch on his next trip to the fields. Until then, he prayed his momma wouldn't notice the frame of her cherished picture was cracked.

After he finished sweeping, Jack asked Lydia to play checkers. 'Best out of three,' Jack could hear his poppa say, but this time Lydia was the better player with bragging rights and she couldn't wait for her momma and Mark to return to tell them.

****

As promised, Mark and Sarah returned to find the house and barn still standing and no arguing taking place. Lydia was sewing and Jack sat reading the newspaper Mark bought in town on the Fourth of July.

"Jack lost two out of the three games we played of checkers," Lydia announced. "Pa would be proud of me."

"Lydia won fair and square," Jack added, never mentioning the frame.

"Yes, Lydia, your father would be very proud of you," Sarah said.

"Congratulations," Mark commented.

****

Later in the evening, as Mark lay thinking of the day's events, he pondered what he must do next. It wouldn't be easy, but he had to tell Katherine in person his life changed and his heart now belonged to Sarah. Making the trip would mean leaving Sarah and the children alone. Sarah successfully handled the last trip when he collected the reward money, but that trip was only five days. He figured this time it would be at least twice that time traveling east to Heather Forks,

Missouri and back.

When Seth Frazer returned from town, Mark planned to ask him if he would check in on Sarah at least once while he was away. He looked forward to Seth's return. Mark wanted to ask Sarah to marry him and what better time to be married than the Fall Harvest Festival a month and a half away.

The following morning, before Sarah called the children down stairs for breakfast, Mark mentioned his plans to Sarah. "Katherine needs to be told in person. I don't love her Sarah. I love you and the children. I must tell her so she can continue with her own life. When Seth returns, maybe he'd check in on you. When he arrives, I'll be ready to leave."

"Are you sure, Mark? Are you sure you want to stay here with us? Sarah slid breakfast off the hot burner of the wood stove and ran to him.

Mark held her in his arms. "I'm determined and my mind has never been more certain of anything, Sarah. I must tell Katherine as soon as possible." He kissed her forehead.

"Yes, it's the right thing to do. You must tell her in person, but please be careful. She may try to pressure you to stay."

Their gazes locked on each other. "Don't worry, Sarah. As soon as she knows the truth, I'll come home, straight back to you and the children." They embraced once more, then called Jack and Lydia for breakfast.

Chapter Twenty-One

As they waited for Seth to return to the farm, there never seemed to be enough hours in a day for Mark and Sarah to be together and it became more and more challenging to keep their promise not to tell the children about their feelings for each other. Mark couldn't resist picking a handful of wild flowers to surprise Sarah. The glances they shared during meals, the smiles that appeared when the other wasn't looking, and Mark coming from the barn to the house earlier for his morning coffee were all telltale signs of their growing affection. When Sarah passed Mark a plate of food, their hands brushed and a passionate connection rippled through them both. Under the table, Mark nudged Sarah's shoe with his boot. A blush lit her cheeks.

How much longer could they keep their emotions from the children? Or, had the children already picked up on subtle changes? Sarah's lighter step and eagerness to please Mark plus Mark's attentiveness to Sarah's every whim made the two of them closer and connected.

****

One evening, while Sarah sat rocking, relaxing after a busy day, she looked at the Miller's house photo sitting on the side table. When she picked up the cherished photo the corner of the frame fell off in her hand. Jack and Lydia were working on their writing lesson when Sarah asked, "Does anyone know how this picture frame got broken?"

Jack looked down at his paper, his facial expression blank. "I don't know," Jack said.

"Maybe it happened the day you and Mark were on the picnic," Lydia said. "Jack swept the house for you, ma. I remember, Jack was only trying to help. The broom bumped the table and I think the picture fell to the floor."

"Jack, do you remember the picture falling." Sarah looked directly at Jack.

"No, Ma, I don't remember." Jack still didn't raise his head or look at his mother.

"Are you sure, Jack?" Sarah gave him one last chance to own up to the truth.

"I remember sweeping that day," Jack finally said.

"You know how much this picture means to me." Sarah walked over to Jack and with her outreached hand raised his head to look at her. "It sat on that table ever since we unpacked it from the Miller's things."

"Well, all it needs is some red cedar pitch to hold it together. I meant to fix it so you'd never notice, but it escaped my mind until just now." Jack finally admitted.

"So, you just lied to me," Sarah said.

"But, Ma," Jack tried to explain.

"No, Jack," Sarah cut him off. "You will not only fix the frame tomorrow, but you will give back your father's knife until you prove you've learned from your mistakes. It's always better to own up to what you've done or what has happened than to get caught in a lie. Usually, one lie leads to more lies to hide the truth, and most times there are consequences for lying. It's better to tell the truth from the beginning."

Head hanging low and shoulders slouched, Jack said, "Sorry, Ma. It won't happen again." Jack handed his momma the knife before climbing the ladder to his bedroom.

"Let this be a lesson for you too, Lydia." Sarah stressed the word lesson.

"Yes, Momma. I understand," Lydia replied in a soft voice.

Sarah didn't notice, but Mark's head drooped too. He was thinking about the lies he told and the consequences they might have one day.

****

A few days passed before Seth Frazer returned from his trip to town. He arrived one afternoon with a wagon full of lumber, a keg of nails, sacks of provisions, and a smile on his face.

Everyone gathered to greet him. The children were eager to hear his news and he was anxious to share. He slid down from the wagon seat and stretched out the kinks in his back.

"Good news," Seth announced. "A woman from my hometown has agreed to come west and visit. Her name is Emily Gibson. We'll see how things work out."

"That's great, Seth." Mark extended his hand. "Happy to help and give you a hand with any heavy lifting or chores."

"No thanks, Mark. I need to do this myself, but I appreciate your offer."

"Okay, Seth, but if you change your mind the offer stands."

Sarah congratulated him next with an embrace followed by a handshake from Jack and a big hug from Lydia.

"Come on in and sit a spell before supper." Sarah offered.

On the way to the house Mark took Seth aside and spoke to him in private. "I have business in Missouri I must attend to immediately. It'll take me away a couple of weeks. Could you check in on Sarah and the children while I'm gone? It's important or I would leave. I'll be back as soon as I can."

"Sure. Happy to help. Don't worry."

"My saddlebags are packed. Since you'll be spending the night, leaving now would give me a head start. Thanks for your help, Seth, and congratulations on Emily Gibson coming west."

Mark took Sarah aside and explained, "Katherine needs to be told and the sooner I leave, the sooner I'll return."

"You have to do this, Mark, but promise me you'll return."

Mark put his finger on her lips to hush her. "My mind is made up, sweetheart. I want to be right here with you and the children." He kissed her and held her close.

Sarah clung to him. When she finally released him she said, "Please be careful and come back to us, Mark."

"Don't worry, everything will be fine. You have my promise, my word." He tenderly kissed her again to reassure her.

Sarah brushed away her tears before she called the children to say good-bye. Seth walked out with them. Jack and Lydia knew Mark was leaving, but of course not why.

"I'll be back before you know it," Mark said,

hugged both children, then twirled Lydia in circles, and shook Jack and Seth's hands. Then Mark walked back to his bunk to retrieve the last of his surprises for the family.

"I want to give you these before leaving." Mark handed out parcels to each child, and one to Sarah as he mounted Ruby. He leaned down and kissed the top of Sarah's head. He couldn't help himself. He knew he would miss her terribly, but knowing Seth would be checking on them eased his mind.

Lydia didn't wait. She opened her package right away. Her eyes lit with delight. "There's enough fabric here for two dresses. Thank you, Uncle Mark."

Jack unfolded his sack and pulled out a coin pouch. "I never had my own coin pouch before. Real cowhide, too." Then he opened it and a coin dropped into his hand. "Look, a shiny Liberty silver dollar." Jack was stunned. "A whole dollar. Gee, thanks, Uncle Mark."

Sarah opened her sack. Inside was a *Godey Ladies* magazine and a bundle of beautiful light blue fabric. "Thank you, Mark."

"You be careful, Uncle Mark," Lydia said.

"Safe travels," Jack added.

Sarah blew Mark a kiss and mouthed the words, 'Be safe. I love you.'

"I'll be back in time to harvest the third cutting of hay. I won't be any longer than I have to." Mark took off his hat and ran his fingers through his hair before replacing his hat.

"You'll see me again as soon as possible. Be good and do your chores for your momma," Mark said and rode off. A short distance down the path, he looked back and there stood Sarah still watching him. He turned in the saddle and waved his hat in the air.

Sarah waved back.

He took one long, last look and galloped off.

****

During supper, Seth explained further about his doings in town, "Did I share with you my preacher put out the word in the east that a man in Kansas sought a companion and would pay her way if willing to make the trip.

"Well, word finally arrived. Emily Gibson from my hometown of Sheffield is interested."

During supper, Seth talked about fixing up the house, and how he couldn't wait for Emily to make the journey. He stayed the night, sleeping in the barn, and awoke eager to return home. "There is much to do and very little time," Seth explained with a pitch of excitement.

True to his word, Seth returned a week later to check on the Clark family, spent the night, helped Jack with the chores and then was ready to leave. "I'm heading to town to pick up a few things," he announced. "I found I needed more supplies after starting projects to get the house in shape for Miss Emily. Is there anything I can get for you, Sarah?"

"You could check for mail from back east for us," Sarah said, "And please, plan on staying the night on your return trip."

"I'm going to stay in town a few days, but I'll rest here on my way back through. See you then." Seth waved and headed toward town and Sarah busied herself in the garden.

As Sarah waited for Mark's return, the hours passed slowly. Every day her heart reassured her, she truly loved him. She said those words to him the day of their picnic. If Mark returned to her and the children, she would show him her love for the rest of her life.

It wasn't the same love she had for Samuel. That love was a once in a lifetime connection and he would always be her one true love. Mark made her feel protected, safe from harm, and gave her a reason to look to the future. She depended on him and welcomed the strength and security he brought that took away the fears that sometimes swept over her; the biggest fear being that she alone would not be able to provide for her children. Now Mark would be there to teach Jack and Lydia things Samuel never had the chance to share.

Sarah loved the fact that Samuel and Mark shared the same values. Mark said he loved her and she believed him. He made her feel alive again. Oh, how she missed his presence, her arms ached to hold him, and she prayed for his safe return.

Suddenly a rush of unbidden thoughts flooded her mind as she cooked breakfast one morning. *He will come back to me and the children, won't he? He says he loves us. He has to come back. He gave the children last minute gifts. He gave me fabric to make a beautiful dress.* She smelled the eggs in the pan begin to scorch and flipped them quickly. *Could they have been good-bye gifts? Would he return or was that a good-bye forever wave as he rode out?* No. She had to stay positive.

Sarah promised herself when Mark did return, she wouldn't ask him any questions about Katherine. If he wanted to talk about her, she would wait until he brought up the subject. She prayed every night he would return to her, so they could start their new life together.

Chapter Twenty-Two

After days in the saddle traveling east to Missouri, a dusty and hungry Mark finally rode upon the sign, 'Heather Forks Settled1832 6 Miles'. Miss Katherine was on his mind. He needed her to understand his new circumstances and release him from their arrangement. He truly cared about Katherine and didn't want to hurt her, but things were different now with Sarah and the children in his life.

Sarah, sweet Sarah. He couldn't wait to ask her to be his wife. He loved the time they spent together and their talks after the children were asleep. Envisioning her smile warmed his heart. Sarah and the children were his new life. Samuel entrusted him to take care of his family, but this had grown into more than just caring. He loved them. As a man of honor he struggled, for he had also given his word to Miss Katherine Weaver.

Katherine would be heartbroken and angry, but Mark prayed she would forgive him in time. He needed to speak to her first and then explain to her father, man to man. Surely Mr. Weaver would be sympathetic to Mark's new commitment and responsibility and help Katherine accept his change of heart.

Mark knew Katherine would never leave Heather Forks. Her father groomed her to take over the Weaver Hardware Store. Mark had taken a part-time job at the store one spring after coming off a cattle drive. The work soon became full-time and Miss Katherine and he became friends. When he announced his intentions to court her, he suspected Mr. Weaver had reservations about him as a suitable match for his cherished daughter.

If Samuel hadn't died, he would be proposing to Katherine instead of wishing Sarah were in his arms. Despite the seriousness of the encounter, it would be good to see Katherine again.

Arriving at Heather Forks before the close of the business day, Mark rode directly to Weaver's Hardware Store hoping to catch Katherine before she left for home. His plan was to ask her to dinner where they could talk, just the two of them, and he could explain about Sarah.

He tied Ruby to the hitching post in front of the store and entered. Nothing had changed. The nail kegs were still full to the brim, tools hung on the wall in the same locations, and the cash register sat on the counter where he expected to see Katherine standing behind it ringing up a customer. He took off his hat and ran his fingers through his hair. Before he could take another step, he spotted Mr. David Weaver, Katherine's father, heading his way.

"Mark," Mr. Weaver said in a surprised voice, "Katherine feared something happened to you when you didn't return at the promised time. Then we got your letter stating you weren't sure when you were coming. And here you are months later. How could you expect her to wait for you this long? A promise is a promise."

Before Mark could explain, Weaver seemed to come to some kind of decision and led him down a nearby aisle. "There's something I have to tell you, son. Why don't you come for dinner tonight? Katherine will be glad to see you. We are all interested in your plans."

"Well, Sir, I do need to talk to Katherine."

"Come for dinner at six o'clock and the two of you can talk then."

"I planned to ask her to join me."

"No, you must come to the house. I insist." Mr. Weaver put a heavy arm around Mark's shoulders and walked him to the door where he said, "I'll let Katherine know you're coming."

Things had not gone as Mark expected, but he stabled Ruby, got a room at the hotel, and cleaned up before setting out to Katherine's home a short distance away. As he rounded the corner of Weaver's Hardware, he was suddenly confronted by three men, their faces covered by bandanas. They viciously leapt upon him, dragging him to the back of the alley.

Mark tried to free himself and got his head slammed into a post for his efforts. A beefy arm encircled his neck from behind and his arms were pinned in a vise grip rendering him defenseless. He tried kicking and thrashing, but to no avail. A mighty blow to his face resulted in a sickening crunch and, tasting blood, Mark guessed his nose was broken. Two hard punches to his chest knocked the wind out of him. Then one assailant delivered four hard thrust at his ribs, a forceful jab to his right eye and two crushing blows to his shoulders. Drained of strength and in shock, Mark fell to his knees. Pain radiated from every pore. He heard the scrap of the blade drawn from a leather sheath. A blur at first, but when it got closer, Mark focused on the shiny blade coming toward him. He tried to jerk his head out of the way, but the knife cut deeply into his cheek. The thug said in a raspy voice, "Here's a scar to match your other one. Katherine Weaver won't look twice at you now. Leave tonight and never return. You're not good enough for Katherine Weaver. Leave now or die tomorrow."

Recoiling in pain Mark tried to call out, but no sound could escape. With a final crushing blow to the head that rendered him unstable, he fell to the ground.

One of the perpetrators gave a final kick to the battered body and the three left.

In a haze of confusion, Mark painfully dragged his bruised and bleeding body to the wooden walkway before he passed out. A passer-by who almost tripped on Mark's outstretched arm looked down at his bloodied and beaten face and shouted for someone to get the doctor. Peopled gathered.

"Why, that's Mark Hewitt," an onlooker said. "He used to clerk at Weaver's store."

"Someone, get Katherine Weaver," another voice called out and a woman who heard the request ran to fetch her.

****

Mark regained consciousness many hours later, lying in a bed in unfamiliar surroundings. Raising a heavy hand, he touched his swollen, bruised face covered with bandages. His eyes could open only a slit. Shooting pain and throbbing muscles kept him from lifting his head. Racked and bruised, he gingerly explored the areas that received the greatest assault.

"Oh Mark, its good you're awake. I brought some soup for you."

Through a haze, Mark heard but did not register the

woman's voice. Pain assailed his body and his head ached unbearably.

"Don't try to talk, Mark, dearest. The doctor said to rest and eat a little if you can. Here, let me help you sip some water. You're safe with me now and that's what matters. Doc gave you a sedative to help take away the pain and let you sleep. I'll be right here with you."

When Mark next tried to open his eyes, sunlight streamed in the window. Where was he? What had happened?

The woman hovering over him spoke in soothing tones, "The doctor said you were lucky. Your ribs don't appear to be broken, just badly bruised. Your nose is broken, but he set it and it shouldn't be too noticeable when healed. He stitched the cut on your cheek and there'll only be a small scar. Oh, and your eye is cut and you have a real shiner, but the swelling will go down in a few days. The doctor was most concerned about the bruise on your head. He said it probably caused a concussion and you should rest. It will be awhile before your ribs heal and you're back to yourself. You'll stay right here until you're mended."

Mark only dimly heard and understood even less of what the woman hovering over him said. His head pounded with pain. He had no idea where he was. He was trapped inside his own body and couldn't find a way out. A picture of a hay field flashed and he heard a woman's voice say softly, "The hay needs to be cut." *The hay? What hay?* Images ran through his head.

"You kept saying Sarah Clark's name last night. I knew you were concerned about her, so I sent off a short note this morning letting her know you're here. I mentioned your incident briefly but told her you'd be fine since I'll be taking care of you from now on. You're home. You're finally home."

Sarah? Mark heard this name as though from a great distance. *Sarah Clark? The name sounded familiar but why?* Confusing images crowded his mind and soon he became drawn back to the comforting darkness that brought him peace.

Awake again, dim light lit the room. The woman sat in the chair beside his bed. Who was she? She stirred, rung out a cloth in a basin, and reached to wipe his forehead. Mark blinked open his eyes for a better look.

"Good you're awake. Here, the doctor said to give you one of these pills to help with the pain." She held his head gently as he drank.

It was all Mark could do to swallow.

"Take a few more sips. You need water," the woman said.

Mark fought to keep his eyes open. He wanted to ask her questions, but once again the darkness overwhelmed him.

The next afternoon, some of the pain had subsided and the haze lifted a little. The woman carried in a tray and said, "You're finally awake. Try a little of my chicken broth. It will help your throat and you need to keep your strength. I don't know the last time you ate." Katherine held the spoon to Mark's lips and he sipped gratefully.

After a few spoonful, Mark raised his hand as enough and closed his eyes. *I have to think,* but found himself again slip into unconsciousness.

The next time Mark opened his eyes, a dim evening light from the window fell across the form of a woman sleeping in the chair. He tried to say something, but only a slight sound escaped, not enough to awaken her.

Awaking again, the room was dark but the woman still sat by the bed. His head was still fuzzy and still hurt fiercely, but snatches of images were beginning to rise. *My body hurts so. Why am I so sore? Oh, I remember something... A blow to my face. I was held down. Did someone hit me? Was I attacked? Where am I and who is this person in the chair next to me? I'm so weak. I can't remember.* He slid helplessly back into darkness.

Chapter Twenty-Three

Minutes seemed like hours with Mark gone. Sarah and Lydia worked sewing dresses from the fabric Mark gave them and cut out shirts for Jack and Mark. They all worked in the garden and caught up on household chores, and even took a few dips in the swimming hole. Sarah carried a knife at all times.

On wash day, Sarah fetched dirty clothes from Mark's bunk in the barn and found herself wishing he were there to wrap her in his arms the way she wrapped his shirt around herself. She pretended he had returned and they were dancing at the Fourth of July Festival, reminiscing of the moment they connected, the moment she knew she loved Mark.

Standing in the creek scrubbing his shirt, she closed her eyes. They told each other their true feeling at the picnic. Mark said he loved her. They kissed and held each other. Oh, how she longed for his touch.

If someone told her a year ago that her life would be turned upside down, she wouldn't have believed them. She'd dealt with two deaths, both devastating and difficult. Now her entire future with Mark lay ahead.

She wrung out the shirts, and when she tossed them in the laundry basket on the shore it dawned on her, Mark hadn't taken much with him, so surely he hadn't planned on being away for too long. Her concerns about his return subsided somewhat and she continued about her days knowing Seth would soon be coming to check on them.

One day Sarah opened the trunk she started packing a few months ago with Samuel's clothes to add his belongings from the bureau. To her surprise, she found several items she'd forgotten about such as the stones Samuel and Jack collected on the wagon train journey west. In each state he and Jack looked for interesting rocks. It gave them something they could do together. She would be sure Jack got them on his next birthday.

She also found a silver cigar case and two sets of cuff links, one gold and one of porcelain that were his father's. Then, way in the back of one drawer, wrapped in paper with writing on it, she found Mary Miller's wedding band. She'd know it anywhere the design tracings were so unique. The note read, 'This is for Lydia. She is such a sweet little girl. Please give it to her on her sixteenth birthday and tell her a story about James and me. Take care of your family, Samuel. I give you everything we own. Good luck to you all. Thank you for everything you have done for us. You are a good man.' It was signed, 'Mary.'

Sarah finished packing the trunk and closed the lid, knowing sometime in the future Jack and Lydia would benefit from its contents.

It seemed no matter what she did or the time of day, her mind always drifted to Mark. He should be returning any day now. *Mark promised. I must have faith. Has it been long enough to ride to Missouri and back yet? He said he'd come home as soon as he could. Faith and trust, I must have faith and trust that Mark will return.*

215

She lost her appetite, her stomach churned constantly and she caught herself in daydreams when she was alone without the children to keep her attention. She would fix Mark the pot roast he enjoyed so much when he returned. They would celebrate and Lydia could make a pie for desert. She and the children would show him all the work they had done. The windows were shinning inside and out and the chicken coop cleaned with its contents worked into the garden soil. Jack caught some fish they smoked and dried, and they all picked berries, made preserves, and dried some for a winter treat.

Keeping the children busy was a full-time job during the day without Mark to help entertain them. Evenings after they were asleep were the hardest for Sarah. She had no one to talk with about the day's events. Drinking her tea alone she'd pick up the Bible and start to read, but her mind would always drift back to Mark. *How much longer would he be away? How would Katherine take the news? Would Katherine let him go without a fight?*

Sarah put herself in the other woman's shoes and could feel her loss. Mark's announcement would hurt Katherine, she knew this, but couldn't help wanting Mark for herself and her children. *Please Mark, please, come home to us. God, please help Mark be strong.*

Chapter Twenty-Four

Days passed by and Mark continued to drift in and out of consciousness. Each time he awoke he remembered more pieces of the puzzle. Details of the attack were sharper now and the pain in his head had subsided.

The woman walked in and began talking.

"Father told me he invited you to supper. You must have been on your way when you were attacked. I hope you can identify who did this terrible thing. The sheriff said he'd come to get a statement when you were able to talk."

Still able only to whisper hoarsely, Mark nodded.

"You keep trying to say Sarah Clark's name. I don't understand. You're with me now. I'm Katherine and you're here to marry me. You can forget about Sarah now."

Hearing the word marriage and Sarah's name together in the same sentence struck a chord in the confusion that was Mark's present state. Sarah. Yes, lovely Sarah, the woman he loved, the person he planned to marry. Then he remembered riding from Kansas to Heather Forks to tell Katherine about Sarah. He must break his connection with Katherine. His heart belongs to Sarah now. Yes, Katherine stood before him. Her voice clearly unmistakable. Then, with a flash, he recalled men wearing bandanas and their last words after pummeling him. 'You're not good enough for Katherine. Leave tonight or you'll die tomorrow.' Overwhelmed with feelings, he slipped back to the darkness.

When he next awoke more details of the vicious attack fell into place. Mr. Weaver asked him to dinner. Staying focused, he reasoned David Weaver was the only one who knew he was in town and when he would be passing by the hardware store. He knew Katherine's father was barely able to hide his dislike of his daughter's suitor and probably paid the men to attack and warn him to leave.

The next day, except for the lingering pain of the sorely bruised ribs and ever present headache, his eye, nose and cheek still hurt, but were improving. He ate real food and was able to sit up on the side of the bed and take a step or two.

"I'm so glad to see you regaining your strength, Mark, dearest," Katherine said. "The doctor's coming to remove the stitches from your cheek and the sheriff wants to ask some questions."

The doctor said, "You're lucky, Mark. Katherine has taken good care of you. You should be back to normal in a few months."

But I can't wait a few months. The hay needs to be cut.

The sheriff asked, "Did you get a look at who did this to you, son?"

Mark shook his head. Without the identity of the three men, the sheriff really couldn't do anything about the situation.

Each day the rib pain eased. He was able to open his eye fully and the facial cut started to itch, a sure sign of improvement. Looking at his reflection in the bureau mirror, Mark wondered if Sarah would still want him with two scars on his face or would the assailant's prediction come true?

I have to talk with Katherine about Sarah. After, I'll be able to head home. My ribs should be good enough to ride soon. My sweet Sarah, she must be out of her mind with worry. I must get back to the farm. The hay needs to be cut. Maybe Seth would help.

But first he had to explain to Katherine and make her understand. He couldn't put it off any longer. The time had come. He had to talk to her.

By the time Katherine brought breakfast the next morning, Mark was dressed, packed, and ready to leave.

"Good morning, Mark," Katherine greeted him. "I'm so glad to see you're up and about. You must be feeling much better."

"Yes, Katherine, I'm feeling well and it's because of you. May we speak please?" He closed the door and sat on the bed.

Katherine put the tray on the night stand and sat in a chair across from Mark.

"Katherine, I must return to Kansas. I didn't think I'd be gone this long. The attack changed everything. I rode to see you in person, because there's something I need to tell you."

"You mean you're not staying?" Katherine tilted her head, eyes opened wide.

No words could take away the sting and hurt Mark was to say next. He prayed the truth was best- painful, but in the end, the best.

"No, Katherine, I'm not staying. I'm returning to Sarah and the children. They need me. And Sarah and I have fallen in love."

Katherine sat up straight in the chair, hands griping the armrests as she choked out the words, "Are you saying you'd rather live on a farm in Kansas with your best friend's wife than stay here with me and take over the Weaver Hardware someday? You've fallen for a farm girl with two children and they are better for you than me? How dare you! How dare you let me care for you and think we had a life together, all the while you lay there thinking about getting back to Sarah and her children?" She crossed her arms.

"Katherine, I am so sorry. My trip here was to tell you in person. I owed you that much. If I hadn't been ambushed, I would have told you after dinner and left the next day."

"Oh, so I'm just supposed to be happy for you? After all the months I've waited and all the promises you made?" Katherine rose from the chair, taking a step toward Mark who also stood, thinking she was going to strike him. "Well I'm not happy." Face red and tears forming she said, "You've hurt me terribly, Mark. If you leave, you'll disgrace me in front of all my friends, the whole town for that matter."

"They'll think me a fool for taking care of you. Is that what you want? You want me to be known as the fool who took care of a man she thought loved her, a man who just ups and leaves for another woman?"

Mark walked over to the window and looked out. "You're angry with me, Katherine. I'm sorry, I truly am. I didn't intend to make you look foolish. No one will think poorly of you, they'll think poorly of me."

Katherine turned abruptly in Mark's direction. "Mark, can you honestly say to my face you don't love me, that you no longer have feelings for me?" She walked closer, her hands clutched in tight fists.

"Katherine, I didn't set out to fall in love with Sarah, it just happened. We share the same values, interests, and we both love her children who now need a father. Please, you have to believe me."

Katherine took one step closer. "I don't care if you planned it or not. I bet Sarah tried to tempt you to stay. She knew very well the position she was in without a man to keep the farm running. Telling you she needed help with the crops was only an excuse to keep you there." She turned away and paced the length of the room, picked up the empty water pitcher, and threw it at him.

Mark crouched just in time. It hit the wall and shattered.

"It wasn't like that, Katherine," Mark implored. "Sarah didn't come to me begging for a husband. I'm sleeping in the barn. The children don't even know we have feelings for each other. I'm here to do the right thing. I rode all this way to tell you face-to-face."

Mark caught her hand as she brushed by and turned to face him. "Katherine, you're a beautiful woman. The men who attacked me said something before they ran off. They told me I wasn't good enough for you, that I should leave that night or be killed the next day."

Katherine stared at him and suddenly sat on the bed.

Mark sat beside her.

She began to sob.

Mark held her until the deep weeping subsided. "I must leave. You hold a special place in my heart, Katherine. You waited for me. No one has ever been so loyal. You'll be a good wife and mother someday. But, I love Sarah and her children."

A tear escaped down Katherine's cheek as she murmured, "But I still love you, Mark. What would make you stay? If you want children, we could have our own children right away. You would be a real father."

"Children aren't the issue, Katherine."

"But, we could run the hardware store together, raise a family, buy some land, build our own house, and…"

Mark cut her off. "Katherine, I admire you and your courage, but my love now belongs to Sarah."

More tears flowed. "Yes, I can see the difference in you. The old Mark wouldn't hurt me like this."

"As much as it pains me to say it, my father probably hired those men to run you out of town. I guess I always knew in my heart he never liked you. I should have heeded his word. He said you'd break my heart one day. I hate him for being right and I hate you."

"Katherine, he loves you so much he can't let you go. I want you to be happy. Find someone who will love you for you, not because you're Miss Katherine Weaver whose father owns the Weaver Hardware Store."

Katherine's tone softened. "Are you sure you can't stay and be that man for me? I love you, Mark Hewitt. I waited for you all these month."

"No, I must leave. I'm sure Sarah is worried and wondering what has happened." Mark stood and threw his saddle bag over his shoulder, wincing a little at the weight and his tender body.

"I plan to leave right away. You'll always hold a

place in my heart." He stood and closed the door behind him on the life that was not to be.

Before riding out, he closed his account at the bank and stopped at the dry goods store. The minute he gazed at the gold band with the small dazzling garnet in the center and a tiny chip on each side, he bought the ring. Sarah would love it too. The jewels represented the three members of his new family.

He had the clerk pack some food for his trip and measure out and wrap three half pounds of candy for the children. Samuel always brought home a surprise from every trip to town. Now Mark understood why and couldn't wait to see their smiles when he handed them the treats.

The next stop was the stables to saddle up and finally set out for home. Mounting Ruby shot a pain to his ribs. Travel would be slow going with many rests. He would ration the pain pills left in his pocket.

As he rode past Weaver's Hardware Store, he looked down the side of the building where the fight took place. As long as the men didn't follow him, he'd be all right.

Riding west into the glare of the setting sun brought a fierce headache. It wasn't until he arrived at the Kansas boarder that he quit looking over his shoulder. Straining in the saddle put pressure on his ribs. Constant pain and the recurrent headaches slowed his journey.

Back in Kansas and grateful the confrontation with Katherine was behind him, Mark's thoughts turned to Sarah and how and when he would ask her to marry him. *It would be perfect if the wedding could take place the day before the Harvest Festival so we can spend our wedding night at the hotel. My ribs should be healed by then.* Joe and Martha Spencer were the only folks he knew Sarah would entrust with the children. He planned to stop at their house on his way home to ask if they'd be willing to help. The third bag of candy the Spencer children would enjoy.

Chapter Twenty-Five

While Mark worked on recovering after his attack, in Katherine's care, Seth returned from town with his supplies and a letter for Sarah. Seeing Sarah at the well, Seth called out, "Only one letter, Sarah. I couldn't help but see it's from Heather Forks, Missouri. Isn't that where Mark was headed?"

"Yes, Mark said Missouri. Would you please forgive me, Seth, if I abandon my manners and read this immediately? It may be about Mark." The handwriting wasn't Mark's. It looked like a woman's script. Seeing his nod, Sarah ripped opened the letter.

August 1858
Heather Forks, Missouri
Dear Mrs. Clark,
I am sending this note to let you know Mark Hewitt is here in Heather Forks. He was on his way to my house when he was viciously attacked by unknown assailants. The doctor said he will be all right in time, but for now he must rest and heal. We are anxious to start our new life together and this is an unfortunate beginning. But I wanted to share with you what happened and reassure you I will take very good care of Mark as he recovers. It is good to have him home at last.

We will be discussing our future plans and making

arrangements for them soon. I look forward to hearing all his stories about his travels and of the assistance he gave you on your farm.

I wish you and your children well with your endeavors.

Sincerely,

Katherine Weaver

Sarah, stunned senseless by what she read, scanned the letter once more in disbelief. *'It's good to have him home? Discussing plans and arrangements for the future?' She wishes me and the children well? Does this mean Mark is not returning and he had Katherine write to tell me they were going to start their new life together?*

A hand to her mouth she stifled a scream. *He promised me. I trusted him. He said he loved me. How can this be happening?* She crossed her arms around her body as pain flooded her being, the betrayal so strong it sucked the breath from her lungs. She gasped for air and turned to Seth.

"Mark's not coming home." Tears welled in her eyes, her head swirled, and her stance wavered.

Seth took her by the arm and led her inside.

"I think I'm going to die." Sarah looked down.

Seth stepped forward to hold her while she wept in his arms. He held her until her sobbing subsided and she managed to step away.

"What is it?" he asked helping her to the chair.

"This letter is from the woman…" She stopped and tried to compose herself. "This woman says Mark was viciously attacked and she is nursing him back to health, and now they can start their life together and that she's glad he's home. She must have convinced

him to stay. I thought he loved me. Now he's gone."
Feeling utterly alone, she clung to Seth's shoulder.

Gently cupping her cheeks, he whispered, "Don't worry, I'm here Sarah."

"I appreciate your help, Seth, but maybe until I hear from Mark I shouldn't give up on him."

"I agree. All right then, first things first," Seth said. "If he's hurt it might take time for him to mend. When we talked, he sounded sure of his plans to return. If he's the man I believe him to be, he'll come to his senses and realize what he's missing.

"We better concentrate on the farm right now. First the hay will need to be cut in a few days. I'll come back and help. I have to take these supplies home and finish a project I started first, then I'll return."

"But what if?" She shook her head. "What will I tell the children? They are so attached to Mark. What if he doesn't return?"

"Don't give up so easy. Remember, first things first. Until you hear from Mark directly I wouldn't mention anything to the children. I'll help out until he gets home. Give him some time. If he's not back in a few weeks, then be concerned. I don't think you have the full story."

Seth left the next morning after breakfast and promised to return by the end of the week to help with the hay.

****

Should I burn the letter from Katherine or keep it? She couldn't bear the thought of Katherine in Mark's arms. *I'll keep it in my bedroom where the children won't find it.*

She couldn't help herself. She read the note at least

227

once a day, praying Seth was right and Mark would return to her, explain everything, and this horrible nightmare would end.

During the day the garden, chores, and dodging question from the children kept her busy. She caught herself snapping at Lydia once when Lydia asked when Mark might return.

Almost a month had passed since Mark left. She couldn't get it out of her mind. *Had Mark lied to me or was Katherine that persuasive?* Exhausted at night from running the farm and helping the children with chores, she thought she could have slept. It seemed like Jack and Lydia wanted her attention every minute. Every other word they said was about Mark and she realized how entwined he was in their lives. Nights were the worst for she had time to think. She must have replayed the day of their picnic a thousand times. Their evening walks, talks of the future and remembering their goodnight kisses gave Sarah some reassurance from her turmoil until she remembered Katherine's haunting letter and crushing doubt returned. Every night Sarah's last prayer asked God to give her strength to carry on and for God to take care of Mark and return him home to her, but tonight's prayer she added, *I'd give anything to have him home again.*

****

Seth returned to help with the hay as promised. She and the children helped Seth cut and stack the hay to dry. After a few days of back breaking work, they stood at the well, drinking cool water when Lydia was the first to hear a faint whooping noise coming from the direction of the fields and she took off running.

Jack ran after Lydia whooping and hollering.

Sarah looking to see what Lydia and Jack are so excited about finally spotted Mark. In disbelief, she rushed to catch up.

Mark waved his hat and Ruby galloped straight toward them.

Mark reined Ruby to a stop, jumped down, and swept Lydia into his arms as Jack hugged his waist and Sarah kissed his cheek and threw her arms around him.

"I'm sorry it took me so long to get home. You're all I thought about when I was gone. I'll never leave you alone that long again, I promise," Mark said, his eyes looking straight at Sarah.

"We have all kinds of stories to tell you," Lydia blurted out.

"Yes, so many stories, I don't know where to begin," Jack added.

"But Mark, what happened to your cheek. You have a red mark." Lydia pointed.

"Yes, it's only a scratch. It's much better now. It doesn't hurt. Come on. There'll be plenty of time for stories later. I see you've been working on the hay field. Did Seth come to help?" Mark knew the answer. They couldn't have done it by themselves.

"Yes, and he's still here. We figure one or two more day and we'll be finished," Jack offered.

"We were just going to wash up and fix supper. I'm sure you're hungry too, Mark." Sarah nudged Jack. "How about you fetch a bucket of water and pull some fresh carrots from the garden? Lydia you start on the potatoes. Mark and I'll be close behind.

The children hurried off and Sarah gave Mark the proper welcome she imagined all those sleepless night. They shared a kiss the likes they had never enjoyed before. Then her hands drifted over the bandages around his ribs. "Are you all right? Katherine's letter said you were attacked. I was so worried about you. I wasn't sure if you'd return to us or not. What happened?" She wanted to know, but the details didn't really matter. All that mattered was Mark returned home to her.

"I'm just fine, now that I'm home with you and the children, sweetheart. It's a long story and I'll tell you all about it later. Katherine said she sent you a letter explaining the attack. I'm sorry she worried you. I took a pretty good beating. My ribs are still tender. Once Katherine nursed me back to health, I left as soon as I could.

Sarah closed her eyes, resting her face against Mark's and a tear escaped.

"Never doubt that I love you, Sarah. Katherine is behind us now. I told her my life changed. I told her I love you and the children. She was upset, but I was honest about my feelings. I couldn't wait to get back to you."

Sarah stretched to greet his welcoming lips, and they kissed again. The passion of the kiss left them breathless, bodies entwined, and eager for some time alone.

"Darling. I'm so glad you're home. The children and I missed you terribly."

Mark wanted to ask Sarah for her hand in marriage that very moment. He held her closer.

Just then Seth saw them and walked over.

Mark extended his hand. A firm handshake welcomed him back.

"I figured you had a hand in getting the hay cut and

stacked." Mark grinned.

"Sarah was concerned you might not be back in time so I volunteered to help. I hope you don't mind."

"Your help is sorely appreciated, Seth. Events delayed my return, but I'll tell you about them later. I'm eternally grateful for your friendship," he said and started toward the barn with Ruby. "Let me get Ruby fed and rubbed down. I'll clean up and come inside."

"Good, I'll fix us all some mint tea." Sarah glanced endearingly at Mark, before heading to the house.

****

After the children climbed the ladder to bed, Sarah and Seth didn't want to miss a word as Mark recounted the story about being attacked, the concussion and its effect on his memory which explained why it took him so long to return.

Seth turned in early and left Mark and Sarah sitting alone at the table to talk further.

Mark took Sarah's hands. "While I was gone I learned how much you mean to me, Sarah. You and the children are the only people who matter in my life. I worried something could happen to you when I was gone." He took Sarah in his arms and kissed her. "I love you, Sarah."

"And I love you, Mark."

Chapter Twenty-Six

The following day, Sarah burned Katherine's letter. Her worry was behind her. As the paper turned to flakes of ash, she prayed for a future with Mark and wondered if that might mean another child in her life. She so badly wanted another child with Samuel, but how could she face the heartache again if something happened?

Seth stayed to finish the fields. Mark was still recovering but managed to help as best he could.

"Thank you, Seth. Without your help with the hay, I don't know how we could have managed. And thank you for looking after Sarah and the children."

"If you need a hand with the corn, just come and get me. I'm glad to help," Seth said.

"Well, I'm going to need you before that, Seth. I plan to propose to Sarah and have the wedding take place the day before the Harvest Festival. Do you think she'll agree to marry me?"

Seth let out a chuckle. "If she doesn't it'll surprise me. She was worried about you when she received the letter from that woman. She actually broke down and cried. She counted the days waiting for you to return. She loves you all right."

"Thanks for telling me this Seth. I'll ask her soon and I'll count on you tending the animals for us." Mark, shaking Seth's hand, nodded a thank you.

Seth readied his gear and rode home to prepare for

Emily due to arrive in October.

There was still much to do before the final harvest and Mark was relieved his injuries were healing without complications. Each day less pain slowed his activities. He and Jack built a small cart out of scrap wood for Sarah to use to carry vegetables from the garden to the house and root cellar. Lydia worked on sewing new aprons from feed sacks for herself and Sarah and mending rips in Jack and Mark's trousers.

Despite working the fields and doing their chores, the children still had time for an occasional swim. Their favorite place was a quarter mile from the house. They asked if they could go, and Sarah agreed a cool dip in the creek sounded good.

While the children and Mark swam, Sarah picked enough wild blueberries for a fresh pie, extra to dry, and some to make into preserves.

The outing refreshed everyone's spirits and the children asked to repeat the event again soon, perhaps with a picnic lunch the next time. Sarah and Mark agreed heartily.

The wood shed, stacked to the rafters, gave Mark and Jack time to finish other jobs like giving the barn a good cleaning and rearranging the root cellar to accommodate more produce. Everyone pitched in and instead of work being a chore, Mark and Sarah made it fun. Jack and Lydia took turns recalling the presidents in order from George Washington to James Buchanan and the date when different states joined the union. While riding in the wagon to haul water from the creek for the garden, they took turns reading aloud from the novels Mark brought them. Slowly, grief for their father gave way to making happy memories.

Mark's plan hinged on Sarah wanting to go to the Harvest Festival. "I would like to go if you and the children want to as well," he said as he proposed the trip. "When we return, the corn will be the last to be harvested."

"Oh, I think the children would love it and we could pick up a few things in town to tide us over the winter."

"That's wonderful, Sarah. If you like, we can tell the children together."

****

Why wait to ask Sarah to marry me? We love each other. We love the children. Maybe there's a chance Sarah will consider having another child. I always wanted a child, even more so since spending time with Jack and Lydia. I just don't know if Sarah could bear trying again. Mark's heart ached to have a child of his own, but he would let Sarah make that final decision.

One thing stood in the way of complete happiness and always surfaced to mind when Mark thought of marrying Sarah. *What about the lies? Keeping my promises to Samuel hasn't been easy. Should I tell Sarah the truth about his death? But telling her the truth would hurt her deeply and that's the last thing Samuel wanted. Telling her would get it off my chest, but would betray Samuel and devastate Sarah. Is it right to start a life with the woman you love knowing you've lied to her? Would Sarah still love me if I told her the truth or would she hate me forever?*

Weighing his options, Mark concluded he couldn't tell part of the truth unless he revealed everything. He couldn't recount the stagecoach robbery without explaining that Samuel shot two men to save the driver and the boy. And he couldn't explain the reward money without explaining the rest of the events.

****

August evenings steadily became cooler as the Harvest Festival fast approached.

As Sarah kneaded bread dough in the kitchen, the children discussed their plans for the trip.

"Someone better ask me to dance this year." Lydia twirled herself around.

"Of course they will, dear. In your new ruffled dress, the boys will be tripping over each other to get in line. You're a lovely young lady with a pretty smile. And who could look away from your halo of red curls after your hair cut? The boys won't be able to resist a dance with you," Sarah insisted. Sarah suspected Jack, if he could get his nerve up, would seek out Abigail, to dance. He never danced with a girl before, only Lydia, and, according to Jack, Lydia didn't count.

"Mark, if you compete in the best-shot competition you should take first place this time," Jack added. "You'll win for sure, Mark. Oh, what I could do with a rifle, Ma. Put meat on the table every night, right, Mark?"

Mark winked at him.

"If you spend all your time hunting," Lydia cut in, "then I'd be left doing your chores too. So don't think you're going to get away with that trick." she plopped her hands on her hips.

Everyone chuckled.

"When we get to town, I'm going to the dry goods store to see the new fabrics," Lydia announced.

"I'm going to the hardware store to look in the gun and knife cases," Jack insisted.

The children's conversation continued with back and forth banter about things they wanted to do and see once they arrived in Dead Flats.

****

After the children were asleep, Mark and Sarah sat at the table to enjoy some barley pudding and a cup of coffee. They discussed things they needed to purchase, as Sarah made a list. Definitely not how he planned things to happen, Mark suddenly said, "Sarah, there's something on my mind. I want to ask you something that concerns us all. How would you like us to become a family...you, Jack, Lydia, and me? What do you think? Can we get married when we go to town?"

"Why, Mark Hewitt, are you proposing to me?" Sarah exclaimed.

"Well, yes, I am," Mark answered without hesitation, "If you'll have me, Sarah. Will you have me? Will you agree to be my wife and marry me?"

"Have you Mark Hewitt? Yes, I'll have you. Let's be married."

Mark stood, grinned ear to ear, pulled Sarah to her feet, and wrapped his arms around her waist.

Sarah returned his embrace, held him close, and gazed into his eyes.

Mark gently raised her to his height and kissed her waiting lips before setting her down where she stood on tiptoe, her arms around his neck, not wanting the kiss to end.

Sarah said breathlessly, "You need to pack your things in preparation for after we're married."

"Unless you'd like to live out in the barn with me?" Mark chuckled, then asked, "Can we tell the children in the morning?"

"Yes, of course, tomorrow, at breakfast we'll tell them the good news."

"Great!" Mark twirled her and caught her in his arms, "We'll leave for town a day early and ask the reverend to marry us. Seth's already coming to feed the animals. We can't have Daisy dry up."

"Seth knows we're getting married?" Sarah gasped.

'Yup, told him before he left." Mark grinned.

"That's less than a week from now. Are you sure, Mark?"

"Yes, I've never been surer of anything, Sarah. I love you."

"I love you too, Mark Hewitt."

Mark leaned down to give Sarah another kiss. He couldn't take his eyes off her. Sarah said 'Yes'. She would be his bride. The words hadn't come out quite the way he expected, but she said yes and nothing else mattered. He wanted to hold her in his arms all night but needed to leave before the urge to stay became overwhelming. Holding her tenderly, he kissed her again gently and then said, "Sweet dreams, darling."

As he looked back for his accustomed last glance, Sarah stood looking radiant in the light of the lamp. He didn't want to leave her. He found it difficult to go to the barn, but knowing he would reside in the house when they returned brought a smile to his face. He smiled all the way to his bed. He couldn't wait to carry his beautiful bride over the threshold. Still, the nagging question haunted him. Should he tell Sarah the truth about Samuel and the money?

****

While Sarah lay in bed, too excited to sleep, she replayed the evening's conversation in her mind. Mark asked her to marry him and she said yes. How would she tell the children the wedding news? Of course they would be happy and accepting of Mark. Still she couldn't settle herself to sleep. After she tossed and turned for what seemed like hours, she understood what she needed to do before she could sleep. She slipped out of bed, found her shawl, and walked to the old elm tree to talk to Samuel.

Chapter Twenty-Seven

After a few hours of sleep, Sarah awoke thinking about Mark's proposal. Her stomach churned with excitement. *In my heart I always knew Mark loved me.*

After talking to Samuel last night, Sarah believed he understood and approved of the marriage. She also talked to him about another child. She remembered he said Mark spoke of children with Katherine. *Would Mark expect a child? God had answered her prayers and brought him back to her. She promised she would give anything if he returned. Could she try again? Would she be strong enough? Could she give Mark a child? Did he even want a child?*

Sarah loved Mark. She wanted to spend the rest of her life with him.

During breakfast, Mark glanced Sarah's way several times. Her cheeks flushed and flutters churned in her stomach. She needed to speak up soon. Jack was anxious to finish chores so he could go fishing and Lydia planned to mend a tablecloth and her momma's apron pocket, torn while gathering eggs.

Sarah began, "Jack and Lydia, before you head off this morning, there is something Mark and I would like to talk to you about." She looked at Mark for support. "As you know, Mark has offered to take us all to town for the Fall Harvest Festival."

"But this will be a special trip," Mark said, then

looked at Sarah.

Sarah smiled and swallowed hard, trying to find exactly the right words. She said, "We both love you very much. And you must know my love for your father will never end. He was a wonderful man, and we all miss him. He will always be with us in our thoughts and memories." Sarah paused, breathed deeply, then looked at Mark and said. "This trip will be special because we"—she gestured toward Mark—"have discovered that we also have love in our hearts for each other. Mark has asked me to marry him. We plan to do this when we are in town. This will make us a true a family."

The children's faces lit with joy. Lydia jumped up and gave her momma a hug and Jack shook Mark's hand, then gave him a hug too.

Lydia stood beside Mark as he said, "I love your mother and I love each of you. Don't worry about me trying to take your father's place. That's not my intention. But, I need to ask each of you if you'll accept me as part of this family?"

Jack looked at his mother. "Ma, we know you and Mark love each other. You tried to hide it, but we knew, didn't we Lydia."

Lydia nodded and a giggle escaped.

"Now we will be a family again. The marriage will make it official," Jack said. "We knew back when Mark picked you the big handful of flowers. Poppa picked flowers for Momma, too. They always made her smile like she is right now. She sure missed you while you were away this trip, Mark. The way you make Ma happy makes us happy too. We accept you, right Lydia?"

Lydia nodded her head vigorously, then sat down and motioned for Mark to sit beside her. Lydia said, "Since we're going to be a family, Mark, do you mind if I call you Father?"

"Yes, of course you can call me Father if that's what you'd like, but I know you'll always remember and love Samuel, as you should." He gave Lydia a kiss on the top of her head and encircled her in a hug which she returned warmly.

Out of the corner of his eye, Mark caught a glimpse of Jack's face. He immediately said, "Jack, if you want to continue calling me Mark, that's all right. Don't feel you have to call me Father."

Jack's tense stance eased. "Mark is all right with me."

"That's fine." Nodding approval, Mark stood and shook Jack's hand, then drew him close for a hug.

Sarah rose and stood beside Mark, putting her hand on his shoulder. "Jack, your father was proud you would carry on the Clark name. He loved you both very much. Jack, you and Lydia will keep Clark and mine will change to Hewitt. Not because I don't still love your father, but because that's what women do when they get remarried."

With a grin and a long sigh, Mark said, "Okay, it's settled. Your mother will become my wife. We'll be a family."

Sarah suddenly placed her hands to her cheeks. "Oh my. With such a short time to plan there's bound to be things I haven't thought of. Oh, I hope it doesn't rain. I'd like it so much if the wedding can take place in the grove by the church." Then she sighed and her hands returned to Mark's shoulder. "Everything will work out just fine, I know it will."

****

They'd take the covered wagon for shade and in case of rain. The wedding would take place when they arrived and the Harvest Festival would start the next day. Questions continued in Sarah's mind as she packed for the journey that would change her life forever. *I'm at peace with Samuel now, but can I handle another pregnancy?*

While Mark and Jack loaded the wagon with water and grain for the horses, Sarah and Lydia attended to the food, clothes, and everything else they might need. The wedding was now the main thought on everyone's mind.

****

After an overnight stay at the old oak campsite with thankfully no accidents at the swimming hole, they arrived in town late the next morning. Mark located their wagon in the shade, under a cottonwood tree next to other families already lined up at the picnic grove.

The wedding drew nearer and he had to make a decision, either shed his guilt or keep his promise. *Samuel should never have made me promise to keep his secrets. Lies have forced me to be less of the man I want to be and are not a good way to start a marriage. But telling the truth now might cause me to lose Sarah and would break her heart for sure. I have to take Samuel's secrets to my grave.* His final decision took away a weight that he'd been carrying for months. Feeling Samuel's approval, he became at peace with his decision. For the first time in a long while, he closed his eyes and thanked God for the peace that now rested in his soul.

****

Wearing their Sunday best, the family walked toward the church to see if Reverend Beckley was available. They found him in the church working on his sermon. Mark introduced himself, then asked, "Would you have time to marry us, Reverend?"

"We want to become a family," Lydia added.

"Why, of course, there's always time to unite a happy and deserving family in marriage," Reverend Beckley said.

"Can we hold the ceremony under the shade of the grove trees out back?" Sarah asked. "I've already chosen the spot."

"Certainly. Let me gather my Bible and find my wife as a witness and we'll join you there."

Sarah led them under a canopy of green along the back of the church to a private alcove. Smoothing wrinkles from their dresses, the bride and her daughter wore the new dresses they made from the fabric Mark gave them before his trip to see Katherine. Sarah pinned the wild flowers that Jack picked for her in her hair. Mark and Jack both tugged at their stiff collared shirts.

The reverend and his wife soon walked around the corner and the reverend introduced his wife.

Mark handed his hat to Jack and ran his fingers through his hair. Jack took off his hat as well. Mark looked at Lydia who stood proud beside her mother. When their gazes met, Lydia winked.

Mark winked back.

With a blue sky overhead, a slight breeze rippled the hems of the dresses, and a strand of Sarah's long flowing hair blew into her face, which Mark gently tucked behind her ear. Lydia stood beside Sarah and

Jack beside Mark.

The reverend cleared his throat and the ceremony began.

Sarah's brown eyes met Mark's gaze. Captivated by the moment, she only dimly heard the reverend until Mark's name was said.

"Mark Hewitt, do you take Sarah Clark to be your wife, in good times and in bad, in sickness and in health, until death do you part?"

"I do," replied Mark, as he pulled the ring out of his coin pocket and gently slipped it on Sarah's finger.

Then Reverend Beckley turned and placed his hand on Sarah's shoulder. "Do you, Sarah Clark, take Mark Hewitt to be your husband, in good times and in bad, in sickness and in health, until death do you part?"

"I do," Sarah said. Looking into Mark's eyes, she held out Samuel's gold watch fob and said, "Mark this was Samuel's, but I want you to have it now. You're a continuation of my love. Samuel will never be forgotten and you will never be forsaken." She slid the fob into his hand and curled his fingers around it.

"I'm proud to wear it." Mark held Sarah's hands in his.

As the reverend said a final prayer, the children stood straight and alert beside the couple. Then the pronouncement, "You are now Husband and Wife."

Mark drew Sarah close and kissed her gently. They thanked Reverend Beckley and his wife for taking time to perform the ceremony.

As Mark and Sarah turned to look at the children, tears streamed down Lydia's cheek. Sarah leaned over and took her hand, "Lydia, are you all right, sweetheart?"

"These are happy tears, Ma." Lydia tried to smile as another tear trickled down her cheek. "We're a new family now, and Poppa would be happy for us."

Sarah held Lydia close and motioned for Jack to embrace them both.

Mark, still smiling from ear to ear, shook Jack's hand and then twirled Lydia around so her new skirt flowed. He took Sarah's hand and the two of them walked a few feet to an old elm where he swept her up, cradled her in his arms and kissed her tenderly. "I love you, Sarah Clark Hewitt. I will always love you," he whispered softly into her ear. He nuzzled his way to her neck and whispered, "I'll never let go."

When Mark set her lightly back on her feet, he said, "Jack, will you fetch the picnic basket and quilt from the wagon, and Lydia, how about you run over and pick out a good spot for us under those trees over there?"

The children scattered.

"Do you know how beautiful you look today, Mrs. Hewitt?" Before Sarah could answer, Mark took her hand and led her out of sight around the corner of the church. Holding her close, he kissed her, then swept her up into his arms again. Sarah laughed in happiness and wrapped her arms around her husband to return his kiss.

Gazing into each other's eyes, Sarah said, "My ring is beautiful, Mark. You never let on and, well...you surprised me."

Still holding her close, Mark answered, "I'm glad you like it. I bought it just for you. The three stones represent our new life together." He kissed her one more time before releasing her.

Then they heard Jack call out, "Where'd they get

to?"

Lydia spotted them as they rounded the corner. "Here they come. Let's spread the quilt right here. This is where we sat for the Fourth of July picnic. This is a good spot for lunch."

After eating, the children scurried off to find friends and Sarah and Mark found they had time alone together on the quilt.

Laying back looking up at the clear blue sky Sarah said, "This is very romantic." She sighed and snuggled close. She wasn't sure how to start the conversation, so she simply shared what was on her mind. "Since my baby died, my emotions have been in turmoil about having another child. The thought of losing another baby is unbearable, but if you want a child, I'd like to try again." Sarah waited in anticipation for Mark's answer.

Mark grinned.

Sarah anxiously added, "You have enough love for one more child, don't you? I know you love Jack and Lydia, but I'd like us to have a baby too."

Before she could speak again, Mark rolled on his side, gently placed his finger to her lips and said, "You don't have to convince me, darling." He put his arm around Sarah's waist and pulled her close.

Sarah wanted to sing with joy to the heavens. She gazed into his eyes and then kissed him ever so tenderly.

Breathless, Sarah suggested, "Let's wait before we share our intentions with the children."

"Let's hope we don't have to wait too long. I love you Sarah." Mark whispered in her ear.

****

When Jack and Lydia returned, Mark announced, "We're having supper tonight at the Wild Rose Hotel. Let's get ready for a special treat."

Before the children scrambled, Sarah took Samuel's knife out of the wagon and gave it back to Jack. "You made me proud today, son, and you've learned from your mistake."

"Thanks, Ma. Lies have consequences and it won't happen again, I promise. I'll take good care of Poppa's knife." Jack hugged his momma.

"I planned this special dinner on the night you said you'd marry me," Mark whispered as the family walked to the restaurant.

Glasses and silverware gleamed under the gaslight chandeliers. They were seated and the specials were announced followed by the exciting selection of dessert. Later, filled with good food served in a memorable setting, they walked outside onto the plank board walkway.

"Couldn't eat another bite," Jack announced. "The prime rib was really good, but the cherry pie was especially tasty."

Lydia said, "The ham and mashed potatoes were the best because someone else fixed them and ice cream too."

****

On their way back to the church grove, several people stopped to congratulate them and offer well wishes. A rush of pride filled Sarah as she stood next to this tall, rugged man who changed her life from despair to one of hope.

Rounding a corner, Sarah literally bumped into Sylvia Turner who, when she recognized it was Sarah curtly said, "Hello."

"Well, hello, Sylvia." Sarah gave a polite smile, then put her left hand on top of Sylvia's and held it for a few seconds longer than would normally be considered appropriate.

"Have you heard, Sylvia? My wedding took place today to this wonderful man standing beside me who loves me and my children. Sylvia, this is Mark Hewitt." She should have stopped the conversation there but couldn't help herself. She added, "And we are very happy."

Sylvia Turner's mouth opened slightly, but no words came out. Then she said in a low voice as Sarah released her hand, "How nice for you. Your work-hand turned into your husband."

Sylvia Turner's opinion wasn't important anymore. Sarah merrily continued on her way, realizing having Mark in her life meant everything she prayed for had come true.

As they approached their wagon, Martha Spencer and her daughter Hannah walked toward them. *That's odd that they arrived a day early for the festival too.* Sarah, excited to tell Martha the news about the wedding and show off her ring, ran to greet them.

"You'll never guess what happened today." Sarah held out her hand to show Martha.

"Well, it's a good thing you got married or we made the trip to town early for nothing. Oh, my. That's a beautiful ring, dear," Martha replied, smiling.

"You already knew?" Sarah asked incredulously.

"Yes, since last month when Mark stopped by and asked if we'd come a day early to watch the children tonight. Of course we said we would. We arrived about an hour ago, and just finished supper. Now you two go. Leave the children with us. They'll be fine and we'll see you in the morning." Martha gave Sarah a hug and released her into Mark's waiting arms.

"There is one more surprise for you, Sarah," Mark said as he handed her a hotel room key.

As they ascended the hotel staircase, it seemed to Sarah as though all eyes were focused on them. She clasped Mark's hand. His callused one intertwined with hers. That touch gave her confidence.

Finally alone on their wedding night, Mark brushed aside a strand of her hair to give her a light kiss on the forehead before closing the door behind them. She had imagined this moment many times. Anticipation mixed with the newness of each other overwhelmed her as Mark held her in his arms. Happiness overcame her and warmed her heart. She made the right decision. This would be a good life. God gave her a second opportunity at love and a chance to give life to another child. After months of tormenting herself with indecision, her heart spoke to her telling her to take the chance. The possibility of giving Mark a child brought a smile to her face. She laid her head on Mark's chest and closed her eyes as their hearts fell in harmony to beat as one.

The night was filled with passionate caresses, loving words, and mutual understanding.

Sarah awoke early, thinking for a moment she needed to get up for chores. Then the radiating heat of Mark's body encouraged her to snug into the closeness of him. She breathed in his scent and relished the opportunity for their time alone.

When Sarah ran her hand softly over his shoulder,

Mark stretched out his arm.

Sarah greeted him. "Good morning, husband."

"Good morning, Mrs. Hewitt, my beautiful bride." He faced her, "Are you happy, my darling?" he whispered.

"I couldn't be happier." Sarah whispered back, snuggled closer and kissed him. "We're starting a new life together." Sarah gazed into his eyes. "You know, Mark, together I feel we can handle any situation that comes our way. I'm so happy you're in my life."

Mark pulled her closer and said lovingly, "And I'm glad you're mine. We'll always be together as we make new dreams."

A word about the author…

Judy Sharer is a historical sweet romance author who has just released *Settler's Life*, the first book in her family saga series titled A Plain's Life.

Judy's series is inspired by her passion for history and the simpler life of settlers, a contrast from her career as a computer programming teacher and Director/Assistant Director of Career and Technical Education.

Judy celebrated retirement by embracing her desire to write. She now writes at her home in the northwestern mountains of Pennsylvania where she and her husband appreciate the outdoor environment.

If you want to know more about Judy and when her next book will be released, please visit her website, https://judysharer.com to receive her newsletter on the next release in her series.

Thank you for purchasing
this publication of The Wild Rose Press, Inc.
For other wonderful stories of romance,
please visit our on-line bookstore at
www.thewildrosepress.com.

For questions or more information
contact us at
info@thewildrosepress.com.

The Wild Rose Press, Inc.
www.thewildrosepress.com

To visit with authors of
The Wild Rose Press, Inc.
join our yahoo loop at
http://groups.yahoo.com/group/thewildrosepress/